Eighteen Roses Red
A Young Girl's Heroic Mission in the Revolutionary War

by
Ruth H. Maxwell

WHITE MANE KIDS
SHIPPENSBURG, PENNSYLVANIA

This book is a work of historical fiction. Names, characters, places, and incidents are products of the author's imagination and are based on actual events.

The acid-free paper used in this book meets the guidelines for permanence and durability of the Committee on Production Guidelines for Book Longevity of the Council on Library Resources.

For a complete list of available publications
please write
White Mane Kids
Division of White Mane Publishing Company, Inc.
P.O. Box 708
Shippensburg, PA 17257-0708 USA

ISBN-10: 1-57249-380-1
ISBN-13: 978-1-57249-380-3

Library of Congress Cataloging-in-Publication Data

Maxwell, Ruth H., 1925-2013
  Eighteen roses red : a young girl's heroic mission in the
Revolutionary War / by Ruth H. Maxwell.
    p. cm.
  Summary: In the colony of New Jersey in 1777, with her family torn apart by the American Revolution, thirteen-year-old Anne Brewster must try to conceal and deliver to General Washington a coded message whispered to her by a gravely injured soldier.
  Includes bibliographical references.
  ISBN-13: 978-1-57249-380-3 ISBN-10: 1-57249-380-1 (alk. paper)
  1. New Jersey-History-Revolution, 1775-1783--Juvenile fiction. [1. New Jersey-History-Revolution, 1775-1783--Fiction. 2. Loyalty-Fiction. 3. Adventure and adventurers-Fiction. 4. Embroidery-Fiction. 5. Farm life-New Jersey-Fiction.] I. Title.

PZ7.M44658Eig 2006
[Fic]—dc22
                                                            2005056259

PRINTED IN THE UNITED STATES OF AMERICA

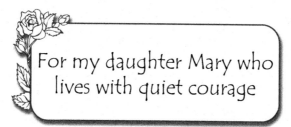

For my daughter Mary who
lives with quiet courage

Contents

Washington's march

Raritan River

Rebel Camp
X

British Camp

Hane's Home
X

New Brunswick

Ferry Landing

Lower New York Harbor

Colony of New Jersey

Map by Author

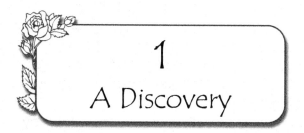

1
A Discovery

Anne Brewster brushed a strand of hair off her forehead. Her face was smudged with soot and her small white cap tilted to one side. She pulled a small shovel from the oven that was tucked high inside the fireplace chimney. Several large black pots hung from a crane over the fire and the house smelled of porridge.

Anne looked at the shovel and sighed. The coals were dark gray and cold. *Drat it!* she thought. The oven was too cool now for baking. She sneaked a look at her mother. Maybe Mama wouldn't notice if she put some new hot coals in.

"Anne Elizabeth," said her mother. "Did you let that oven get cold again?" She shook her head. "Whatever am I going to do with you? I give you one small chore and you fail me. Always with your head in the clouds woolgathering."

"I'm sorry, Mama," Anne said. "I just got so busy with my needlework that I..."

"That needlework will be the death of us all. Well, there'll be no bread today." She put down the pestle

1

she had been using to crush dry herbs and smoothed out her apron. "Can I have your solemn oath that you do all your chores today and be up at dawn tomorrow to get that oven ready for baking?"

"Oh, yes, Mama. I promise. I'm so sorry about today. I sometimes get to worrying about Ben and Adam so far away with General Washington. And all the hateful talk about Rebels and Loyalists. Oh, I hate this war! I know I need to be a better help for you, and I am trying."

Mama sighed. "It's our own fault the way we let Papa spoil you. We've no time for foolishness now, Anne. The war has already taken its toll on this family." Her voice broke. "Oh, go on. Just make sure your chores are done and then you can do your needlework. But don't forget your promise about tomorrow."

Anne picked up her pocketbook and attached it to the waist of her apron. "I'll be so good tomorrow you won't even know it's me." She took off her slippers and put on boots. Then she picked up a small cushion and the linen sampler and raced to the door.

Mama smiled. "Ever our darling Annie."

Anne hurried outside. The sun was still quite high and the sky empty of clouds. *Spring is coming,* she thought as she hurried up the hill behind their log home. Anne loved seeing the colors of the sky and the grass. Small flowers were beginning to show. She looked down at her drab gown. Ever since this war she'd had to wear ugly, stiff homespun. She hated it.

As she walked she looked over her shoulder to the town of New Brunswick off in the distance. That's what she was stitching onto the linen, the whole town, the Meeting House, homes, and gardens. *I'll enter it in the town faire,* she thought. *They can't refuse me that. And*

I'll win. No one's ever done the town before. She squeezed her eyes tight and clenched her fists. *I've just got to win!* The winning stitchery would hang in the Meeting House for all to see, and it would have her name on a brass plate beneath it. Then maybe Cousin Faith would forget all that nonsense about Rebels and Loyalists and be her friend again. Then people would forget Anne's family was a Rebel family. Maybe they would come and help Mama with the heavy chores.

She found a smooth spot near the top of the hill and sat down. She spread the piece of linen onto the grass and sighed. The church steeple was finally finished and now she could start stitching the gardens around the town square. She smoothed the linen carefully.

Anne looked past the rolling green hills of the New Jersey Colony toward the village of New Brunswick. From up here you couldn't tell there was a war going on. It was as if the rebellion had never begun. She sighed. That rebellion had caused her family so much trouble. Her brother Adam, who at sixteen was only three years older than she, had been among the first to take up a musket and join General Washington's army. And then her brother Ben, who was a man of twenty, had gone. She missed him terribly. He was the one who had carried her on his shoulders when she was little, who was always rescuing her from Adam's teasing. Ben was the serious one, so careful in all that he did.

Her brothers had left when the snow was still on the ground and the days were filled with idle hours. "I'll be done and home in time for spring plowing," Adam had boasted. His blue eyes had seemed to dance with joy.

Ben had neither laughed nor boasted. "Keep yourselves safe," he had said. "These troubles will soon be over."

Now it was spring, and the war was still going on. Oh, how Anne wished she could have gone with them, but she was stuck at home doing her stitchery and helping Mama.

Anne reached into her pocket and felt the smooth shell of a horse chestnut. Her face warmed as she traced the carvings *AEB & MJ* with her fingernail. Morgan Jones had carved it for her. Morgan Jones with his wide grin and unruly black hair. Last summer he had slid the chestnut into her hand. She felt warm all over just remembering. Even though it was Cousin Faith who had run after him, showing off in her fancy dresses, it was Anne he'd given the gift to.

A tiny dark fear entered her thoughts. Had Morgan given a chestnut to Faith also? She gasped. That would never do! Anne sighed. If she could win the contest everything would be all right again. Then Morgan and Faith would come and they could picnic again. Maybe they could even...

"Anne Elizabeth Brewster!"

Anne jumped. Mama called her like that when she was angry. Quickly Anne folded the linen and stuffed it into the pocket she wore tied around her waist. She gathered her thread, scissors, and thimble, and jammed them into the little pouch also. She picked up the cushion she'd been sitting on and tucked it under her arm. *What now?* she wondered as she hurried toward her mother's voice. She'd done all her chores. What could it be?

She ran down the hill. "Yes, Mama, I'm coming," she called.

Mama was standing in the doorway of the shed, her hands on her hips. "Young lady, when will you ever grow up and be dependable?" She brushed a wisp of hair from her forehead and tucked it into her cap. "There isn't time anymore for your childish nonsense. What with your father dead and your brothers gone..." Her voice faltered.

Anne swallowed hard as she watched her mother and remembered how she used to be before the troubles began. Mama had loved to dance and had gone about her chores humming favorite tunes. Now Mama looked pale and thin, the music and joy all gone.

"I'm sorry, Mama. What did I do?"

Her mother shook her head. "It's what you didn't do." She pointed to a crock on the shed floor.

"The milk!" Anne gasped. She'd been so eager to get back to her stitchery that she'd forgotten to put it into the stream to cool.

"Yes," Mama said wearily. "And the sow got out again."

Mama had warned her over and over to be sure to latch the shed door so Maybelle wouldn't get out. Tears gathered in Anne's eyes. "I'm sorry, Mama. I truly am. I won't do it again, I promise."

Mama wiped her face with her faded apron. "You said that the last time." She stared at her daughter and sighed. "It's my own fault," Mama said, almost to herself. "I let Ben spoil you. He was always doing your chores, helping you, making excuses for you, waiting on you hand and foot. Adam told me I should put a stop to it."

"But, Mama, he helped Adam too."

Mama sighed and smoothed her apron with her hands. "Well, it's done. No use crying now."

Anne sniffled loudly and her mother frowned. "You can't be the baby anymore, Anne Elizabeth. It's time to grow up and be a woman." She pulled a piece of rope from the shed wall and handed it to Anne. "Go get the sow. She's probably in the woods."

Anne looped the rope over her shoulder and headed toward the wooded hill. Her throat ached with her tears. She'd promised Papa last year before he died that she'd be a comfort and a help to Mama. When Ben left, she had pleaded for him to take her along. "I could carry a musket," she had cried. "I'm near as good a shot as Adam."

Ben had laughed and tousled her hair. "You stay and help Mama, and do your needlework. That will be your contribution." Then he had sobered. "You can't go where I'm going, or do what I'll be doing." He'd fingered the sleeve of her heavy linen dress. "The homespun is drab, is it not? Well, soon life will be again as it was and I'll buy you and Mama pretty dresses of silk." He'd kissed her cheek, and then he'd gone.

She remembered promising him she would be good, and here she'd gone and failed Mama again. It seemed she couldn't do anything right, except the stitchery. She knew she was the best at stitchery. Everyone had said so. Even Aunt Elizabeth and Morgan's mother had admired the piece she'd entered in the last stitching contest. If she could be good at stitchery she could be good at other things as well. She lengthened her stride. Surely the sow hadn't gotten too far away.

"Spring is almost here," she said aloud, pretending Ben was beside her. "And I am trying." The sun was warm and Anne breathed deeply. The air smelled sweetly of damp earth and new growth. She looked at the tiny flowers and lambs ears peeping through the new grass. "I miss Cousin Faith," she said aloud.

On days like this, Anne and Faith had played in the meadow, making crowns of daisies and chewing sour grass. But the rebellion had changed everything. Their last picnic had ended in anger. Ben, Adam, and Morgan had been with them and the talk had turned to politics. "Things are not always as they seem," Morgan had said.

Adam had leaped up and shouted. "You cannot disguise the manner in which these Colonies have been treated."

"That's Rebel talk," Faith said, "and I'm weary of it. Rabble-rousers and ruffians! That's what you Whigs are."

"Aye!" Adam shouted. "That's what I am. A Whig—a Patriot."

Faith looked at him. "Why can't you learn some manners like your brother Ben?"

Ben had become strangely quiet. "If we lose our Mother Country we'll be as orphans adrift on this vast sea."

"Aye," Adam said. "Then cut me loose. This orphan can fend for himself."

"But what of your responsibility to those of your family? What of Mother? Of Anne?" Ben asked.

Anne had bristled. "I'll not need looking after."

Ben reached over and took her hand. "Perhaps not, little one, but what of the farm?"

Anne had seen a look of pain cross Morgan's face and he rose to leave. The party was over. *This dratted revolution!* she had thought. *It spoils everything.*

"My heart grieves for you," Faith had said when she and Morgan left. Anne rubbed her hand against the rough fabric of her skirt as she remembered. Sadness fell like a weight on her chest. Morgan was probably with Faith right now—Faith in her pretty silken dresses, her hair curled with pink ribbons. Tears smarted Anne's eyes. Morgan Jones used to sit with Anne in church and walk through the square with her. Morgan was the one who had carved their initials in the horse chestnut. She sighed. Those happy times seemed a million years away.

Anne and Mama didn't even go into town to visit with anyone anymore. Not since Papa had died. She remembered the last time she and Papa and Mama had gone to church. They'd hitched up the wagon and ridden bravely into town.

"Traitors!" Colin Andrews had shouted, and a rabble of rough boys had followed them, shouting out, "Rebels! Tar and feather the Whigs!"

Morgan Jones had been in the crowd. Morgan who had asked to carry her packages just a year ago. Anne felt her jaw tighten as she remembered.

A ball of mud had hit Mama's bonnet, but she'd held her head up proudly. "Pay the Tories no heed," Papa had whispered sharply. Anne's face burned at the memory of the ugly words. *Why did it all have to be like this?* she wondered. *Oh, why couldn't it all be the way it was before?*

They hadn't been to town again. Ben sent them supplies and Malcolm Drew came with gifts of food and town gossip from his mother. Malcolm was sympathetic to their need. He was one of the secret society, the Sons of Liberty, like Papa had been.

No one else cared to come to visit. Ben was working with Uncle Tobias and sent supplies out every week. There was always a letter from Faith—all full of news of Morgan. "Morgan and I went walking." "While Morgan and I were in church..." "Morgan and I..." Anne dug her hand into her pocket and felt the horse chestnut beside the linen stitchery. Had she lost them both? Without Morgan and Faith her needlework was all she had now. That, and Mama. But Mama was sad and angry most of the time.

"Our cause is just," Papa had said, but that didn't help when the horse went lame. Uncle Tobias's threats had stopped others from coming to help them. So they had not been able to do the spring plowing. They had only Mama's garden and no crop for selling.

If only I could fight, she thought. *I'd help put those Tories in their place all right*. She closed her fingers about the horse chestnut. *How could Morgan have turned against me?* she wondered. Maybe Faith had won him over. At the thought, Anne's heart felt cold.

At the top of the hill, she stopped and looked at the distant town. Threads of pale smoke drifted up from the chimneys and it looked so peaceful. But Anne knew the countryside was filled with Tories, still faithful to the King. She shivered. She knew what they did to Rebels.

Glancing over her shoulder as she climbed the hill, she saw their small house and shed with its pen for the cow. Everything looked so peaceful from up here. She had been born in that house, and Ben and Adam, too. Papa had built the first room before he got married. He'd bought twenty acres with the money his father had left him. He and Aunt Elizabeth had come to New Jersey from Massachusetts because the land was cheap. Then Aunt Elizabeth had married Tobias and moved into town.

Papa had stayed on the land, growing wheat, barley, rye, and flax. "I'm a simple man," he'd said, "a farmer. I love this land and want it to be free of all oppressions."

Mama loved the quiet of the country but she wasn't interested in politics. Anne remembered their last dinner with Aunt Elizabeth and Uncle Tobias. The talk had turned to politics as it always did. Mama had gotten up from the table. "I'll let Papa attend to that," she had said. Her gardens and family were her loves and she tended them well. Aunt Elizabeth, Uncle Tobias, and Faith had often been treated to her produce and flowers.

Uncle Tobias had sputtered at Papa, "Foolish politics is all you attend to. I've heard the talk." He shook his finger at Papa. "You've been going to those secret meetings."

The room became so still Anne dared not even breathe.

"Tobias," Papa answered, "a man must live by his principles and beliefs. You are loyal to the King because he pays for your bread. I am loyal to my land and to my fellow citizens."

Uncle Tobias's face had turned bright red. "You're not too proud to have your son Ben work for me and earn his bread from the King."

Papa had nodded. "Ben is a man and has a right to his own beliefs. But I can no longer live under a tyrant. These Colonies are weary of supporting the King's wars. We are being bled to death with unfair taxes and I'll do what I can to see that it stops."

Tobias had leaped from the table, knocking over his chair. "Sir," he said, "leave this house. You and your family are not welcome here. You are an enemy of the King, a traitor."

They had left. Faith had run after Anne and taken her hand. "Oh, Anne, you could come and live with me."

Anne had shaken her head. "No, I belong with my family."

"At least you could dress better. Homespun is so drab and ugly," Faith said. "I won't be seen in it. It's certainly not fitting garb for a lady." Papa started the wagon. "I'm not a Patriot but I'll write to you," Faith called after them. "Please write back."

The very next day, Adam left to join Washington's army and Mama had cried for a week. Ben sputtered and fumed away at Papa to make up with Uncle Tobias. When that didn't happen, Ben had turned silent. Finally, he'd left, saying he was going to do what he could to end the troubles. Then the Tories had captured Papa one evening as he rode home from his secret meeting. The beating had been serious and Papa had died.

Anne's face burned at the memory. Oh, if she could just see Uncle Tobias. She'd give him a tongue-lashing. And then Anne remembered Papa's words. "Don't you be revengeful, Anne girl. That'll just sour you. We do what we have to do. I have to live by my convictions. Tobias lives by his." Oh, how she missed Papa. She'd gotten her blue eyes from Papa who had been so strong and who was glad she was a girl. He'd taught her to read and write. And even though Mama had fussed that it wasn't proper for a young lady, Papa had shared all of his political pamphlets with her, even some of the secret ones. Anne still had them. He'd taught her all of the verses written by Phyllis Wheatley, the slave who wrote poetry. Anne was Papa's favorite child, and everyone knew it.

Anne felt a pain in her heart. No wonder Mama was so sullen and unhappy. She missed Papa too. And she was lonely. Aunt Elizabeth hadn't come to Papa's wake or funeral services. Her own brother! She hadn't even written a note. *Oh,* Anne thought, *I'm wool-gathering again, just like Mama says I do. But I'm going to change,* she promised herself. *I'm going to grow up and be dependable like a soldier. No more bawling like a baby. I'll be a Patriot like Papa was.* She quickened her pace.

The shadows stretched long in the afternoon sunlight. Anne squinted her eyes, looking for Maybelle. The sow couldn't have gone far. She was soon to have a litter and the added weight made her slow and irritable.

A glint of sunlight caught Anne's eye and she gazed up into the trees as she ran. The dark green of the leaves against the pale sky pleased her. *Someday we'll wear silks again, not just the rough homespun fabric.* Anne knew that wearing the homespun showed that her loyalties were with the Rebels and not with the King. *But after the war we can use fine linen again and I'll get enough for a coverlet,* she thought, *and I'll mix the blue and green of the shadows.*

Suddenly, she spilled headlong and landed spread-eagle on the ground.

"Oh-h-h," someone moaned.

Fear paralyzed Anne. She turned slowly. A young man was leaning against a large oak tree, his face pale in the shadows. On his right shoulder was a brown stain with splashes of red, and clutched in his hand was a musket.

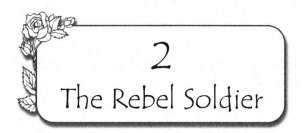

2
The Rebel Soldier

Anne scrambled to her hands and knees and stared at the man.

"Don't go," he whispered. "I need help."

She rose slowly and backed away. "The sow...," she croaked. "Maybelle...I have to find the sow." Her legs trembled.

"She's here somewhere," the man said. "I saw her..." He coughed, his body jerking uncontrollably.

He's hurt bad, Anne thought, but she couldn't move. She'd been warned about British runaways and spies. Maybe he was pretending so he could rob them. Or kill them! Her eyes widened in fear and she stepped backwards.

"Don't go," he said weakly. He leaned back against the tree, his face twisted in pain. "I won't hurt you, I promise." He coughed again. "I need doctoring. I have an important message."

Anne didn't move. "You could be a Britisher, just pretending..."

The young man tore open his homespun waistcoat. "Does this look like a British uniform? Miss, you've got to

13

believe me! Find Daniel Brewster or Malcolm Drew. They will know me."

Anne gasped. "Papa!"

He interrupted. "What?"

"I'm Anne Brewster. Daniel was my father."

The young man sighed. "Take me to him. I've an important message for him." A trickle of fresh blood spilled down his chest and he dropped his musket and slumped forward.

Anne rushed toward him. "You're hurt bad."

He nodded. "Help me, please..." His eyes closed.

"Mama," Anne whispered. "She'll know what to do. I'll take you home to Mama." Gently she put her arm about his slim waist and his arm over her shoulder. Then she pulled him up so he could stand. He wasn't much taller than she was. "You'll have to walk, but it's not far."

The man leaned heavily on Anne as she led him home. Once, he stumbled, crying out in pain. His blood spilled warm onto her hand. Anne felt her legs shake as she steadied him. "You've got to keep going. We're almost there," she said as they stumbled down the hill. "Almost there, almost there," she chanted, a promise to them both. And soon they were on the path beside the shed.

"Mama!" Anne called. "Mama, come quick!"

Mama stuck her head out of the door and frowned. She wiped her hands on her apron and hurried outside. "Anne Elizabeth, what have you done?" Mama placed her hands on her hips. "Aren't we in enough trouble?"

"But, Mama, he knows Papa. He's a Rebel soldier, Mama, I just know it, and he's got a message for Papa, and he's been shot, and oh, Mama, do you think he'll be all right?"

"Why, he's just a boy," Mama said as she studied him. "Not much older than Adam."

The young man moaned.

"Oh," Mama said, "he's bleeding in a bad way." She put her arm about the soldier. "Let's get him into the house before he swoons."

They helped the soldier limp inside and lifted him clumsily onto the bed.

"Poor boy," Mama muttered as she placed her hand on his forehead. "He's burning up with fever." She pulled his muddy boots off and tossed them into the corner. "Did anyone see you?"

"No. I don't think so."

"Pray no one did. I'll need hot water and a poultice." When Mama pulled the shirt away from the wound, the young man moaned.

Anne gasped at the raw, gaping hole. "Don't hurt him, Mama," she pleaded.

"Lead's gone clear through," Mama said softly. "That's a blessing. I'll clean the wound." She turned to Anne. "Did you get the sow?"

"No, Mama. What with the soldier, and..."

"Go get her," Mama whispered, "I don't aim for us to starve next winter. And hurry back."

Anne couldn't take her eyes off the man as she backed away. A Rebel soldier was there in her house. He didn't look like a soldier. This man was plainly clad in rough leather trousers and jerkin. He was wearing a homespun shirt like the one Adam had worn when he'd gone off to war. Anne wondered what the Rebel uniforms looked like. The British soldiers had bright red uniforms and tall fancy hats. Anne felt a thrill of fear race through her.

She picked up some oatcakes as she walked past the table. Maybelle loved them. Then Anne ran out of the house.

The sun was disappearing as Anne entered the woods. She shivered in the evening air. It would soon be night. She sneaked a glance to either side. *Was the soldier followed?* she wondered. Suddenly, she bumped her toe against a rock. "Ow," she cried, and then bit her lip. No more tears, she promised herself. There was too much to do. This was her chance to prove she was grown up and that she could be depended upon. She thought of her promise to Papa. She had to grow up quickly if she was to keep it. Now was her chance to not only comfort Mama but to help her as well. She would help with the soldier. That would be a real contribution to the war. She ran farther into the woods.

The rope was right where she'd dropped it, and the sow was nearby, snoring softly as she slept. Anne looped the rope around the sow's heavy neck. "Come on, you fat old thing. We've got to get home."

The sow snorted and struggled to her feet. The soldier's musket was lying in the grass. *I've got to hide it,* Anne thought. She picked it up and was shocked at its weight. Ben had always helped balance the musket for her when she shot at targets. She tried to hoist it to her shoulder, but it was longer than she was tall, and she had to use both hands to keep it there. That would never do, for she had to lead Maybelle home. Yet, she couldn't leave it. They might have need of it. Adam had taken theirs with him to war. Finally, she looped the rope around her wrist and cradled the long musket in her arms.

Anne talked to the sow all the way home, telling her about the soldier and his wound. "He knows Papa.

Says he has a message. It's important, he said so. Maybe it's about the war." She shivered at the thought.

Maybelle stopped suddenly, jerking Anne's arm. "Oh, Maybelle, don't be so stubborn. We've all got to be brave. You too." She held a piece of oatcake out in front of Maybelle and soon they were on their way again.

It was dark by the time Anne reached the shed. The pale glow from the windows in the house comforted her. She pushed the sow into the shed, hung up the rope, and leaned the musket against the wall. "Now, you stay put," she told Maybelle, and gave her the last of the oatcake. Then she closed the door and latched it. She wasn't going to be careless anymore.

The house was warm as she stepped inside and the sharp smell of sulphur wrinkled her nose. Mama burned sulphur to purify the air whenever there was sickness in the house. Anne looked at the man in the big bed. They'd moved the bed into the sitting room when Papa was sick and had just left it there. Since no one came to visit, Mama said she didn't care anymore. Besides, it was warmer in here during the cold winter.

The young man's face was ashen and still. "Is he..." Anne couldn't finish the sentence.

"He's sleeping," Mama said without raising her head. She was peeling potatoes and turnips and dropping them into a black iron kettle. "I'll make him some broth. I wish I had a piece of beef, but this will have to do."

"Did he tell you about the message?"

Mama nodded.

"Did you find it?" Anne asked.

Mama shook her head. "His clothes will need washing. I put one of Papa's nightshirts on him. Poor lad. He's bad off. I wonder where he comes from—if he has a family."

"But the message..."

"There was no paper on him," Mama said. She hung the heavy kettle onto the hook and swung it to the back of the fireplace.

"He must have it in his head," Anne said thoughtfully. "He said he had an important message to deliver."

"That well may be, but the lad's in no condition to deliver anything. I'll have to sit up with him."

"Oh, let me," Anne begged.

Mama studied her. "You remember what happened with Papa," she said softly.

Anne's face flamed hot at the memory. She'd begged to sit up with Papa for a spell, and when Mama had let her, she'd dozed off. Papa had wakened in the night, out of his head with fever, and had fallen out of bed. Ben had heard the noise and come to help. Dear Ben, he was always rescuing her and taking care of her. But Ben was gone. Anne straightened her back. "Mama, that was almost a year ago. I'm older now, and besides, didn't I get him down the hill? Please, Mama."

"You'll have to bathe his face with alum water to bring down his fever."

"I know how."

"And call me if anything seems amiss."

"I promise."

They busied themselves making their supper of bread and beans. Anne washed the dishes and then brought in wood for the night. She checked the water bucket. It was full.

Mama tucked a strand of hair behind her ear. "Poor lad," she whispered. She looked at Anne. "I'll sleep in the loft. Be sure to call me if you have need." She looked over at the young man. "Wonder who he is? Who his folks are? We might never know."

Anne shivered. "I'll call if I have need."

"Very well," said Mama. She brushed Anne's cheek with a kiss. "I'll leave two candles burning. Do your needlework. It'll keep you awake." She walked away. "I'll look for nettles tomorrow," she called out. "We'll need a decoction to draw out the poison."

Anne nodded and hurried over to the large bed. The soldier had almost disappeared in the feather comforters. His arms were over the faded coverlet with his hands folded. Anne sucked in her breath. Papa's arms were like that in his coffin. She leaned over and put her hand over the soldier's face. He was breathing! Relief spread through her. She moved the big chair so she could see him and also have light from the fire. Then she placed the candles on a nearby bench and put the basin of alum water beside them. She dipped a cloth into the cool water and wrung it nearly dry. She'd seen her mother do this often. Gently she wiped the man's brow. He stirred and muttered, "Griffin...garden."

Anne leaned over. "Yes?" But he only moaned a reply.

She put her hand on his chest. His heart was beating, slowly and faintly. She wiped his wrists and hands, then sat in the big chair and watched him. He was so still. His breathing didn't even move the coverlet. His fair hair was damp and curled softly on his face. *He looks like Adam,* she thought, *only older.* A feeling of compassion flooded through her. Adam might be the worst pest this world had ever seen, but he was her brother and she cared for him.

The soldier moaned. Anne leaned over him. *He's so sick,* she thought. *Maybe he's even dying and there are hundreds like him, working and dying for the cause.* She wondered about his family, his mama and papa. Maybe he even had a younger sister. The thoughts became too much to bear and she shook her head. *I must think of other things,* she said to herself, and she picked up her stitchery.

Pale gray moonlight filtered through the window and Anne moved the candle closer. She would stitch the gardens on the fabric now, rows of flowers and vegetables, all colorfully in bloom. She wanted the colors to be beautiful and happy, the way life used to be.

The man stirred and Anne dropped her needlework and moved to the edge of the bed. His eyes were open, glazed with fever and pain. "Where's Daniel Brewster?"

"Papa's dead," Anne whispered.

The soldier closed his eyes and moaned. He grabbed her arm and pulled her close to his face. "Malcolm Drew. Get Malcolm...I've a message." His eyes closed and opened again. "Message," he whispered, "four days...for General Washington...it must get through."

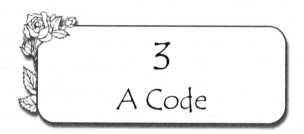

3
A Code

The soldier struggled again to sit up and fell back against the pillow.

"Please don't move," Anne pleaded.

He gazed steadily at her and Anne could almost feel the strength of his look.

"I've got a message for General Washington. He's nearby..."

"Oh," Anne interrupted, "he can't be or we'd have heard. My brothers Ben and Adam..."

"I've got a message," he said again, and his voice quivered. "There's still time...and oh, Mother, the wheat crop's in...The general..."

Anne gasped. *He's out of his head,* she thought, *the way Papa was when he was dying.* She pulled herself free.

The soldier looked at her again. His gray eyes seemed dark and foreboding. "The general moved the troops and now they're coming," he whispered. "The British...in four days...to New Brunswick..."

Anne gasped. That was only a few miles away.

The soldier closed his eyes and then forced them open again. "Washington's army is west of New Brunswick southwest of the ferry, and he needs to know." His eyes closed again.

"But....," Anne stammered, a jumble of thoughts racing through her mind. Ben and Adam were with Washington and now they were nearby. But why hadn't Ben sent news? And what if the man was telling the truth? Fear knotted her stomach. Quickly she wrung out the cloth and patted the soldier's clammy face.

His eyes fluttered and he grabbed her wrist. "Where's Malcolm?"

"In town."

"Is there anyone here who can get the message to him?" His voice was intense and the words felt like arrows hitting her chest. "Will you?"

Panic tensed Anne's body.

He struggled again to sit and she saw a new red stain on his bandages. *He's bleeding again,* she thought. She tried to free her arm, but his fingers dug into her wrist and held her fast. Anne was amazed at his strength. He pulled her close to his face. "If Malcolm doesn't get the message through to Washington," he whispered fiercely, "they'll all be killed."

Anne gasped. If he was telling the truth, her brothers would die. Not Ben! Nor Adam! They can't die. But what could *she* do?

His fingers tightened. "Will you go?"

Anne stared at the ashen-faced man. His eyes seemed to pierce right through her.

"I...I...Yes!" The words seemed to explode from Anne. "I'll go. Easy now. Just be quiet," she said.

He let go of her arm and fell back onto the pillow. "Have you a writing instrument?" His voice was a whisper now.

"Yes."

"Get it."

Anne glanced toward the loft where her mother was sleeping and hurried to the chest-on-chest. Carefully she opened the drawer where her father had kept the quills and felt inside. The inkpot was there but it was caked and dry.

"Miss," the man said urgently.

"I'm coming," Anne whispered. She poured a few drops of water into the inkpot and stirred it with the handle of a wooden spoon. She picked out the best quill and then frantically looked around the room for something to write on. They hadn't had any paper about for ages and she wouldn't deface Papa's pamphlets. The fabric left over from the bandages was lying crumpled on the bench. She grabbed it and spread it out on the bench. "I'm ready," she said softly.

The soldier struggled to focus his eyes. Beads of perspiration glistened on his forehead. Anne felt her heart leap. He looked so feverish.

"Write what I say, in this order," he said.

"Order?" Anne asked.

"Yes, just as I say it you write. Understand? Every word."

Anne nodded. "I understand."

"It's just that it's so important." He coughed. "Ready?"

"I'm ready."

"The garden is planted. Eighteen roses red, stocks of blue." He spoke slowly so Anne could write. "Hollyhocks and primrose, sweet William two. Canterbury bells with lilies white. Rows of carrots and cabbage to greet the light. And the password is Griffin."

"Griffin," Anne repeated softly.

"Now, repeat it back to me."

When Anne had finished, he closed his eyes. His face looked calmer now, but oh so pale. "Miss," he whispered, and Anne leaned over to hear. "Promise it will get through."

"I promise," she whispered back.

He closed his eyes and sighed deeply.

He's dying! she thought. She pulled back the coverlet. The wound was still staining the bandages a deep red. His body was damp with sweat. She put her ear to his chest and was shocked at how clammy he felt. She held her breath and listened. His heart was beating unevenly and fast.

Quickly, she wrung out the cloth and bathed his chest and face. Then she covered him again. She sat down and sighed. Why had she ever promised to deliver that message? It didn't even make sense. Besides, Mama would never let her go into New Brunswick alone. The town was filled with Tories. Anne went cold at the thought of what they might do to her. She'd heard about the Rebels they had tarred and feathered and dumped outside of town. She shook her head. It was nonsense, just pure nonsense to even think about it.

Anne jumped when a log crackled loudly in the fireplace. The shadows seemed ominous and she imagined a British soldier in every corner. Chills moved up her spine. She looked toward the loft where Mama was sleeping. *Poor Mama,* Anne thought, and felt an ache in her heart. Mama missed Papa so much, and the boys too. With no one to do the heavy work, Mama and Anne had both worn their hands raw putting in the garden. As hard as they'd worked they hadn't done even half of what Papa and Adam used to do. She couldn't bother Mama now. She needed her sleep.

Anne took out her stitchery and began to sew. Stitching always quieted her nerves. But the thoughts in her head refused to stop. *I promised,* she thought, and immediately the thought *I can't* rose up. *But the British...in four days.* Anne shivered. She couldn't even think about that. *I'll have to go,* she thought. *But, I can't.* Back and forth, like a seesaw, the thoughts flew until she felt she'd go mad. Finally she could stand it no longer. She walked over and quietly opened the door and stepped outside. The air was crisp and smelled of wet dirt. The moon was nearly full.

Anne walked out into the garden and looked up at the hill toward Papa's grave. *Oh, Papa,* she thought, *what should I do?* She thought of Adam, always playing tricks on her and teasing her about Morgan. And Ben. At the thought of him her throat tightened. "Oh, Papa," she said aloud. "What should I do?" Papa always had answers for her. No matter how busy he was, he always stopped and listened. "What should I do?"

She could almost feel her father's calloused hand on her shoulder. "There's my girl," he'd say. Anne knew about the Sons of Liberty and how dangerous it was to participate. Adam had told her all about it. She knew that when Papa sneaked off in the night he was taking messages to others. Papa wouldn't hesitate for a moment to take the message. That's why the Rebel soldier was looking for him. Tears filled her eyes. She thought about Adam. He'd do it and be gone like a flash. Then she thought again of Ben, her older brother. He'd been almost like another father to her. Shy Ben, with his big hands and feet. He'd gotten so quiet and cold before he'd gone. She closed her eyes with the ache of loneliness for him. The thought of anything happening to him was more than she could bear.

Anne went back into the house and closed the door. She put a log on the fire and tiptoed back to the soldier's bed. He was still sleeping. She dipped the cloth in the alum water and wrung it out. Gently, she wiped his face and neck. Then she stroked his arms and hands and covered him. She sat down in the chair and picked up her needlework. She had a lot to do. She thought of the contest. Her stitchery just had to be chosen. When it hung in the Meeting House, Morgan would see it there. Maybe he'd come to call again.

Anne had decided to use a burden stitch for the fence around the graveyard. She was sewing with a dark thread to underlay the open pattern. When finished, it would be a colorful stitchery of New Brunswick town. She'd even put in Faith's house. She loved making the stitches; she could imagine all sorts of fanciful things. Her mind would wander down all kinds of interesting paths. In her daydreams she was dressed in beautiful gowns, and Morgan was always beside her.

She heard the soldier sigh and looked up. She was not imagining now. This was real. The war had come right into their home. She glanced at the cloth she'd written the message on. He had said all of the information was there. She could carry that in her pocket. But what if a Britisher captured her? He'd find it and know it was a code and hang her as a spy. Everybody knew about codes. Even Anne knew about secret codes. Anne's mouth went dry at the thought. She couldn't do that. Again a jumble of thoughts filled her mind and she stitched even faster. She'd just have to memorize the code. She closed her eyes and said aloud, "The garden is planted. Eight roses red..." She peeked at the message. That wasn't right.

For several minutes she tried to learn the message by heart, but she was too excited. And what if she mixed it up? He said it had to go in the right order. What could she do?

She threaded her needle with a strand of scarlet silk that Ben had included in his last package. It was the color of the British grenadiers' uniforms. She stared at the silken thread gleaming in the pale light and a marvelous idea came to her. Of course, she thought, she could carry the message with no one the wiser. Quickly, she began to stitch.

By dawn, Anne's eyes burned with weariness. She knotted her thread and leaned forward to bite it off. A stab of pain shot through her back. She was stiff all over. She spread the linen out on her lap. The stitches weren't as fancy as she would have liked, but the French knots and running stitches had been faster. Besides, she could do it over later, when she got back. The stitchery was crude and yet alive with color and design. She folded the fabric and put it into her pocket and then stretched her cramped hands. The piece of homespun she'd written on was lying on the bench. She couldn't let Mama find it, not yet. She grabbed it and looked at the fireplace. She probably should burn it, but they had so little fabric now. She stuffed it under the straw-ticking mattress. There would be time later to do something about it.

A dove called softly from the meadow and Anne looked at the window. It would soon be day. She stirred the fire and moved the kettle of water nearer the flames to heat. Her eyes burned with weariness and she yawned.

Mama came into the room, smoothing down her hair. "It's near day. I really slept. How is he?"

"He's sleeping," Anne said.

"You must be bone tired. I was sure you'd call me. Why don't you get a bite to eat?"

"Later, Mama, after the chores." Anne put her hand on the soldier's forehead. His breathing was shallow and uneven again, and his skin hot and clammy. "He's shivering, Mama, and yet he's burning up."

Mama nodded. "I'll make a poultice and pack the wound again. If his blood gets poisoned, he'll die." She shook her head. "He's mighty sick, poor thing." She turned. "Come, Annie, my dear, work is good for worry. Eat a bite and then go milk the cow."

But Anne couldn't eat. Her stomach was a bunch of knots. She rushed out to the shed and dragged the musket into the horse's stall, laid it down, and covered it with straw. It would be safe there.

She leaned her head against the cow's warm flank. "I'm scared," she whispered. "But I promised I'd go with the message. And I've got to make it all right with Mama to let me go. Somehow, I've got to." She pulled the stool out and got the pail from the shed wall. The cow's udder was warm in her hands and the milk hit the pail noisily. "Go...go...go....," it seemed to say, and a tingle of excitement rushed through her.

4
Mama Says No!

Anne finished her milking and put the jug in the stream to cool. Then she went to look for eggs. She thought about the Rebel soldier and wondered what his name was.

She found two eggs and hurried inside. Mama was at the soldier's bedside, wrapping his shoulder. She was frowning in her concentration.

"Eggs, Mama. The hen is laying again," Anne said. "Maybe you can make a pudding for the soldier."

"He'll not be eating pudding. Least for a while." Mama lifted the young man carefully.

Anne rushed to the soldier's bedside. He was deathly pale.

"We'll boil the soiled cloths," Mama whispered as she tied off the ends of the bandage. "I fear his blood's beginning to poison."

Anne held her breath. "But he'll live?" she asked.

Mama sighed. "We'll do what we can. Poor soul. I'd want someone to do the same for my boys." She carried the soiled bandages to the fireplace. "I should burn them," she muttered, "but we've little cloth left. We'll boil them."

Anne remembered the piece of fabric she'd written the soldier's message on. It was still hidden under the mattress. She reached beneath the mattress and pulled it out. Mama shaved a few pieces of soap into a kettle and filled it with water. Then she hung the kettle on the long black crane that swung over the fire. "I've got to get some nettles, and some willow bark," she said. "And a web or two. You'll have to stay with him just till I get back. Then you can sleep." She picked up a dark shawl and wrapped it around her shoulders. Then she dropped a knife and a roll of damp linen inside a basket.

Anne brought the cloth to her mother. "Here, Mama. We can boil this too."

Her mother frowned.

Anne held out the cloth. "It's a message, Mama. He told me in the night. I think it's a code."

At the word her mother froze. "Code!" she sputtered. "Code! I'll hear no talk of such things. Not anymore. It's brought us only grief and trouble. Anne, the countryside is filled with people still loyal to the King." She shuddered. "You know what they'd do to us if they thought..."

"But, Mama..."

"Quiet, Anne. No more talk of codes. Talk like that destroyed this family."

Anne's eyes burned with unshed tears. Mama was right. It was Papa's words that had angered Uncle Tobias and Morgan's father. Those words were carved in her memory. "Let Britons in England submit to be governed by fools, but American Britons will ever be free." Then Papa had quoted Tom Paine to them and said, "I love the King and our brethren in Britain, but I love freedom more. I pledge my life and my fortune to our cause." Uncle Tobias had been furious. "Traitor!" he had shouted. "Leave my home and don't come back until you've rid yourself of your poisoned ideas." They had left, but Ben, always the peacemaker, had stayed behind to smooth things over. The following week Ben had moved into town.

"But, Mama," Anne said quietly. "Papa said our cause is just. And Ben..."

"Just!" Mama's eyes blazed. "What good is that when a husband is beaten so that he dies? What good to have your sons taken from the bosom of their family? To be abandoned..." She glanced at the soldier. "That could be Ben or Adam." She wiped her eyes with her apron. "I'll have no more talk of justice or causes in this house ever again."

Anne had never seen her mother so angry. She watched wide-eyed as her mother gathered up her basket and headed for the door.

Anne spoke quietly. "The soldier says General Washington is nearby."

Mama shook her head. "Can't be so or we'd have heard. Ben and Adam would have sent us word. He's out of his head with fever." She opened the door. "You mind him well. Make some gruel. We'll all have need of it." She stepped outside. "And get any foolish notions about codes out of your silly head." She slammed the door.

Anne stood motionless. How could Mama talk like that? Didn't she care about the war? About Ben and Adam?

The young man cried out and Anne rushed to his side. "The British...the British," he called. He tried to rise. "Grenadiers...Griffin..."

"Sh-h-h," Anne said. She dipped the cloth in the alum water and wrung it out. She wiped his face and neck and then his slim arms and hands. He tried to open his eyes, but failed.

"It's all right," Anne said. She sat in the chair beside him and watched until he quieted and finally slept.

She checked his breathing. It was shallow but even. Anne got up and went over to the table. She measured out the cornmeal and put it in a three-legged pot, then she ladled in water. She pushed the pot into a corner of the fireplace and banked it with pieces of wood. *What am I going to do about Mama?* Anne thought. She had promised to deliver that message to Malcolm Drew.

She glanced at the soldier. He had said Papa's name. Daniel Brewster. They were the only Brewsters in the county. And Malcolm Drew. "The Widow!" she said aloud. Of course. She could take the message to the Widow Drew. Malcolm was her son. He'd know what to do. Anne busied herself tidying up the room, humming softly. It was going to work out.

The door opened. "You're mighty cheerful," Mama said.

Anne smiled.

Mama's basket was filled with nettles. She dumped them into the kettle of water hanging over the fire. Then she carefully placed the damp piece of linen on the table.

Anne peered at the cloth. A spider's delicate web lay across the fabric. "Looks like lace," Anne said.

Carefully, Mama rolled the web into a tiny ball. "Lace to cure the poison." She carried the pellet over to the bedside. "Bring me some spring water," she called to Anne.

Anne filled a dipper with water and brought it to her mother. "Lift his head," Mama said.

Gently, Anne slipped her arm beneath his shoulders and raised the young man a few inches. Mama slipped the pellet into his mouth and then gave him a sip of water.

The man swallowed noisily. "Message," he whispered. "Promise."

Anne lowered his head. She had to convince Mama. She just had to.

"The Widow Drew," she said.

Mama frowned.

"The soldier said he knew Malcolm Drew. I could take the message to the Widow Drew. Malcolm will know what to do."

"What message? Anne, this is..."

Anne interrupted. "Mama, last night he gave me a message and I promised I'd take it."

"Anne, I've already told you..."

Anne hurried on. "Mama, he says General Washington is west of New Brunswick. I could walk into town and be there by supper. The Widow lives on the edge of town. No one need see me."

"This is pure foolishness."

Anne stood tall. "Mama, I can do this. You know I can. I won't take the road. I'll be careful. I'll stay with the Widow and be home tomorrow eve. I promise." She paused. "You've got to let me go. You've just got to. It's what Papa would want. It might save Ben and Adam."

Mama's eyes filled with tears and she turned her face away. "Papa filled you with his Rebel talk. You and Adam. Well, I've lost a husband and two sons to it. I'll not lose you. You'll go nowhere, young lady."

Anne was stunned. Slowly, she walked to the hearth and stared into the flames. She slipped her hand into her pocket and felt the stitchery. It was safe.

She watched as Mama tended the soldier, and a resolve began to flood her body. That young man had been wounded trying to get the message to Papa. Now Papa was dead. Anne gritted her teeth. *Someone has to go,* she thought, *and it's going to be me.*

5
Anne Leaves

Anne found a small basket and put in three seed cakes and a heel of bread. She covered them with a pale yellow cloth. Then she hurried into her room and pulled the stitchery from her pocket and spread it on her bed. The garden was still there, the roses and sweet William. It hadn't been a daydream. Carefully, she folded the fabric and tucked it deep into her pocket beside the smooth-shelled horse chestnut.

She opened her dower chest at the foot of the bed and brought out a dark green knitted shawl. The evening would be cool and she might have need of it. Quickly, she slipped off her felt slippers and pulled on heavy stockings and her boots.

Anne walked over to her clothes press and opened the door. She peered at herself in the tiny mirror inside. No time to rebraid her hair. She smoothed it as best she could. Then she put on a clean white cap and tucked the ends of her dark hair inside. Her hair was the same color as Ben's. Not fair like Adam's and Papa's. She and Ben had the coloring of their mother, except Anne had

Papa's blue eyes. Anne looked closely at her eyes. Morgan had called her "Miss Blue Eyes" the day he gave her the horse chestnut. Again she reached into her pocket and felt it lying smooth and safe within.

Anne looked once more into the mirror. *I'm going*, she thought. *Really going*. She hoped she wouldn't see Morgan or Faith. It would hurt too much if they snubbed her. She closed the door of the clothes press and hurried into the other room.

Mama was stirring the gruel. "Are you chilled?"

Anne fingered her shawl and nodded.

"Don't you get sick now. Best get some sleep. You look tired."

"I'm fine." Anne's voice felt choked. *I must act normal,* she thought, *so Mama won't suspect.* "I saw lamb's ears and spring grass yesterday."

Mama smiled. "Spring is most welcome."

"I'll go get some herbs and greens for our dinner."

"'Twill be a pleasant change from our usual fare," Mama said.

Anne picked up the little basket. "Well," she said, "I'm off."

Mama didn't look up.

A tiny fear tugged at Anne's heart. She hurried over and hugged Mama.

"Run along, child." Mama said as she shrugged her shoulders. "We've work to do."

Anne dropped her arms and looked at the soldier. "Will he be all right?"

Mama glanced at the young man and sighed. "He's in God's hands now. I'll do the best I can." She looked at Anne. "I think you should sleep. You look so drawn."

Anne shook her head. "I'm fine, Mama, really I am." Her mind was racing with thoughts. What would Mama do when she didn't return right away? She had to leave her a message. "Is there a piece of cloth I might have?"

"Whatever for?"

"Ah...I want to try some stitches."

Mama frowned. "There's a bit of homespun in my basket by the hearth."

Anne found the piece and took it to the bench where she'd left the ink and quill. She looked back to see if Mama was watching. She wasn't. Quickly, she penned *Had to go. Home tomorrow eve. A.*

She put the quill and inkpot into the drawer and shut it. Then she glanced about the room. Where could she hide it so Mama would be sure to find it?

"What are you dallying about for, Anne?"

"I'm going," Anne said. "I just wanted to look at the soldier." She laid the cloth on top of the soldier's body. Mama would find it there. Anne wondered what Mama would think when she read it. Anne sighed. She hoped she wouldn't be too angry. "I'd best go."

"Check the garden on your way. Something's been nibbling at the new growth."

"I will." Anne opened the door.

"'Bye, Mama."

Mama nodded and kept on stirring. Anne closed the door and hurried down the path. She was on her way. Twice she looked back, but no one was there.

At the top of the hill, Anne walked over to Papa's grave. They had buried him here, on the land he had so loved. It had been his last request. "Bury me beneath that tree," he'd said. "You know the one." It could be seen for miles, a fitting marker for him.

Anne stood at the foot of the grave. "Well, Papa," she said out loud. "I'm taking the message and Mama doesn't know." Her voice cracked. "I have to go. I left her a message. I'm going to the Widow Drew's. She'll tell Malcolm and he'll know what to do." She sighed. "We miss you, Papa. Mama's not been the same since you've been gone. There's little joy for us now."

Tears crowded into Anne's eyes and she sniffled loudly. Then she straightened her back. *No time for weeping*, she thought, *there's work to be done*. "Well, Papa, I'm on my way. I'll see that Malcolm gets the message." She turned away and headed toward town.

Within minutes, she was on the road. Anne walked briskly, her arms swinging at her side. Her long legs covered the ground easily. Thick white clouds rolled high into the sky and a tiny worry tugged at Anne. They could mean rain. She pushed the worry aside. She'd be in New Brunswick long before the storm broke.

The soft green of spring was everywhere. Anne looked about and memories of happier times flooded her mind. The hours she'd spent tagging along after Ben and the picnics she'd had with Faith. She remembered when Morgan Jones had first come. He'd thrown acorns at them and made himself a general nuisance. Anne felt herself blush as she remembered his grabbing her hand and squeezing it. She'd acted angry, but inside she had been thrilled. *How could he have changed so?* she wondered. She slowed her step and felt the familiar gray sadness creep into her thinking. They had had such good times together, she and Faith and Morgan, and now...*This will never do*, she thought. *I've got to pay attention to what I'm doing.*

She looked down the road. It was empty, but she'd heard of the British deserters. Men who had tired of army rations and restricted life and roamed the countryside stealing and making trouble. No woman was safe. Quickly, she hurried onto a nearby path.

A crow swooped down from a tall tree. His raucous voice startled Anne. Fears for her safety and thoughts of Morgan raced around in her mind. *I'll go mad if I keep this up,* she thought. She had to think about other things.

She and Faith used to recite poems. Papa had copied some of Phyllis Wheatley's from a book and Anne had memorized them. Her favorite was the one about General Washington.

"Thee, first in peace and honour," she said aloud. "Fam'd for thy valour, for thy virtues more, Hear every tongue thy guardian aid implore!"

She frowned, trying to remember the next line. "Hear every tongue thy guardian aid implore!" she said slowly. Then she brightened.

"Proceed, great chief, with virtue on thy side, Thy ev'ry action let the goddess guide. A crown, a mansion, and a throne that shine, With gold unfading, Washington! be thine."

Little had she realized when she'd learned it that someday she'd be on her way to help him. *Great chief,* she thought. *Rebel chief!* "Rebel," she said the word aloud, then looked about quickly to see if anyone had heard. There was not a soul in sight. She laughed. "Rebel!" she shouted, and the word boomed out over the quiet countryside.

From out of the grove ahead, a husky man stepped out. "Rebel. Aye, miss, that I am."

6
The Deserter

Anne stopped still, her heart thumping loudly in her chest. "Who are you?"

A crooked smile flashed over the man's bearded face. "What you said, a Rebel." He started walking toward her.

Anne studied him carefully. Behind a scraggly beard his face was thin and pale. His waistcoat was tattered homespun—he could be a Rebel. Then she saw the soiled red breeches. *A deserter!* Goose pimples started at the back of Anne's neck. "Where are you from?" she asked.

The man continued walking slowly toward Anne. "Who are *you*?" he asked, "and where are *you* from?" He kept looking at her basket. "What's a lovely young miss like you doing out alone?"

"I'm going to my uncle's," she lied. "He's sending a carriage and some soldiers for me. I thought I'd surprise him and meet him halfway." She stood on tiptoe and looked over the man's shoulder. "He should be along soon."

The man laughed. "I'm certain he will be." He stepped closer. "Got anything to eat in there?" He pointed to her basket. "We could have a cozy little picnic."

Cold fear filled Anne at the man's tone. He was not to be trusted and she knew it. She slipped the basket from her arm and held it swaying in her right hand. When he was close enough, she shouted, "Take it!" She threw the basket as hard as she could into his face and raced past him.

Behind her, she heard a curse and then a laugh, but she didn't stop. She ran until her breath burned her lungs. But she did not stop. She ran, too fearful to even peek behind to see if he followed her.

She was running up the hill near McNabb's brook when she stumbled. "Ow!" she cried, as her knees and hands hit the ground. She got up and brushed herself off, and looked at the road behind her. No one was in sight. The palms of her hands smarted and she pressed her fingertips against the bruises. Her legs were trembling and her throat felt hot and dry. She walked over to the brook. She scooped up water from the clear stream and drank thirstily. Then she put both hands into the cold water. She kept them there until the throbbing stopped. Her stomach rumbled and she thought of the basket of food she'd thrown at the deserter. The memory of the man made her shudder. Goose pimples crawled down her spine.

She heard a dog bark in the distance. *Probably from the McNabb place,* she thought. They were still farming, even though the Tories had done their best to get rid of them. She remembered the night the Tories had burned the McNabb barn. That was the night they had set upon Papa. He was on his way home from one of his secret meetings when they had jumped him. Papa had gotten away but had been badly hurt. He'd collapsed when he got home. Adam had grabbed the musket and headed for the door. "Damned Tories!" he'd said. "They'll pay for this."

"Adam!" Papa had commanded. "Stay. Hold your temper. There'll be a way...your day is coming. Patience, son. Patience." And Adam's day had come and he'd gone off to war. And poor Papa. Tears filled Anne's eyes. He'd gone to his bed that night and never recovered.

Anne lay back on the ground and glanced toward the West. The clouds were thicker and darker now. She was tired and hungry. Maybe she should stop at the McNabb farm for a bit. Someone there might be able to help. And then she remembered. Just the McNabb womenfolk were left, the girls younger than she. *I've got to get going,* she thought. *I promised.*

Anne sat up and thought about Ben. She imagined him in a uniform. It would be blue—a brilliant blue, with cords of gold braid over the sleeves and shoulders. The British grenadiers were dashing in their scarlet and gold. She wanted the Rebel soldiers to be just as dashing. It would make going to war so much more pleasant. She took another sip of water and then stood. *Private Anne Brewster better get going,* she thought. She looked down at her simple frock of drab homespun linen. *Some uniform!* she thought as she hurried back to the road.

The way was longer than she remembered. When she walked this way with Morgan and Adam, the time seemed to fly. Adam had always been with them, it seemed. He teased and made jokes, so full of life. She wondered what he was doing now that he was a soldier. Probably entertaining the other soldiers. And Morgan?

What was he doing? Did he ever think of her? She wondered if Faith missed her at all. As difficult as Faith had become this last year, with her superior airs, she had been Anne's best friend. Faith had many friends, living in town as she did. But Anne was isolated in the country. She had depended on the visits from Faith and Morgan. And now no one came to visit her.

Anne felt her chest get heavy again with sadness. This would never do. She had to think about other things. She'd think about another poem, but this time she'd be quiet. She'd take no more foolish chances. But what could she recite? She thought through the things she'd learned at Dame School. They were dull. Mama's verses were always about being good. She smiled remembering one Adam had taught her. He had made her promise never to tell Mama. It was one of Philip Freneau's patriotic poems. Mama would be furious if she knew.

"From the scoundrel Lord North, who would bind us in chains," she said under her breath.

"From a dunce of a king, who was born without brains...From an island that bullies, and hectors, and swears, I send up to heaven my wishes and prayers, That we, disunited, may freemen be still, and Britain go on—to be damned, if she will!"

She felt a thrill go through her. Mama would never allow her to say that word. Even Papa wouldn't like it. "Damned," she whispered and again looked about. She was getting closer to town. She'd best be careful. She left the road and followed a path.

It was mid-afternoon when she reached New Brunswick. Most of the day was now gone. The Widow Drew's house was on the outskirts of the village. Anne ran behind a shed and looked about. The Widow's house was on the next street over. She looked to the right and then left and started around the corner.

"Hoy, lads," a man's voice shouted.

Anne pulled back and glued herself against the shed wall. She heard a scrambling sound and then voices. She strained to hear but caught only an occasional word. "Round-up." Mutter, mutter. Then "King's men." She heard a loud shout and then running. The sounds drifted away.

Anne waited and listened so hard she hardly breathed. The only sounds were a lamb bleating in the distance and the soft lowing of a cow in the shed. She peeked around the corner. No one was in sight. Quickly, she hurried over to the Widow's street. She ran until she saw the familiar dark gray house. At the bright blue door she stopped, and pounded loudly. The Widow was getting deaf.

The door opened cautiously and Anne saw a crisp white cap and then a bright blue eye in a wrinkled face. "It's me," Anne shouted. "Anne Brewster."

The Widow Drew looked up and down the street, then she opened wide the door and pulled Anne inside. "Come in, child...come in," she whispered and slammed the door.

Anne sighed. She had made it.

7
The Widow Drew

Anne stepped into the dark, crowded room. The fire was low and Anne noticed the ashes were piled high. She wondered why Malcolm hadn't removed them. Food and dishes cluttered the table.

"Widow Drew," Anne shouted.

"I'm not deaf, child. Don't shout so."

"But I thought...," Anne sputtered.

Widow Drew smiled. "I just pretend, dear. The Tories think I'm a dotty old woman. Serves my purposes well to let them think so. So don't be put off if I seem a bit daft."

Anne looked puzzled and the Widow laughed.

"You would be amazed at what you can learn when folks think you're deaf. The soldiers speak freely around me. After all, what can an old fool of a woman do?" She lowered her voice. "They would be struck dumb if they knew." She frowned. "But why have you come? Are you alone? Where's your mother?"

"Home."

"Home! Anne, these are dangerous times and you shouldn't be about. Whatever was your mother thinking to let you come."

"She doesn't know I'm here."

"Doesn't know! Anne, how could you? Well, we'll get you right home. Your mother must be frightened out of her wits."

"I've come to see Malcolm," Anne said firmly. "I've got something very important for him to see."

The Widow frowned as she studied Anne. "Malcolm's gone," she said softly.

"Gone!" Anne blurted. "But he can't be."

"Yes, dear. He's gone off to Philadelphia with John Hart. Mr. Hart's our Delegate to the Continental Congress, and Malcolm has been asked to go and help him."

"The what?"

"Continental Congress. They are the gentlemen that are conducting the business of these Colonies. What need have you of Malcolm?" the Widow asked suspiciously.

"He has to take a message to the general's camp." Anne's voice cracked with emotion and she took a breath to try to steady it. "I've got to get this message to General Washington. The British troops are moving."

"Lower your voice, child." The Widow peered at Anne. "Wherever did you hear that?" she whispered. "Where would you get a message for the general, a slip of a girl like you? Who have you been talking to?"

Anne took a deep breath and poured out the whole story. Then she brought out the linen and showed the Widow her stitchery.

When she had finished, the Widow jumped up and hugged her. "You clever girl."

Anne tried to respond, but her words disappeared into the Widow's plump shoulder.

Widow Drew sat down again. Tears gathered in her eyes. "Have we sunk so low," she whispered, "that even our children..." She didn't finish, but shook her head. Her gray curls jiggled beneath her white cotton cap. "Your poor mother," she sighed. "All the mothers." She brought out a large linen square and blew her nose loudly. "Does your uncle know about this?"

"Uncle Tobias? No! He's a Tory."

The Widow nodded. "I know. His office has become a source of trouble. Who else knows?"

"Only Mama, but she didn't believe me." Anne perched on the edge of the bench. "We've got to get this message to General Washington," she said.

"I know you have a message and I'm sure it's important. But you just can't go traipsing into the camp alone. No telling what could happen. Now, let me think. I know," she said, "I'll make us a cup of tea. I think better with a teacup in my hand."

The Widow bustled over to the fireplace. "Please don't mind the clutter. I've been too busy elsewhere to take care of my own home. A cup of tea will do us both good." She lifted a kettle from the fire.

Anne nervously fingered her apron. She folded her stitchery carefully and put it back into her pocket. Widow Drew took a long-handled dipper and slowly poured hot water into the china teapot. "Just herb tea, I fear, I'll have none of the British brew. There is no sugar. But the tea is hot. You look like you have need of something."

She went to the sideboard. "Are you hungry, dear? I don't have much but you are more than welcome to what I have."

Anne thought of the seed cakes that had been in her basket. She shivered as she thought of the man who had gotten them. A faint rumble of thunder sounded, and a knot formed in Anne's stomach. They must hurry.

Widow Drew filled a plate with small buns and slices of dark bread and put it on a wooden tray. She placed cups, saucers, and the teapot on the tray, picked it up and turned to Anne. "I've got an idea. We'll go into my sleeping room," she whispered. "It's warmer and out of hearing of the street." She shook her head. "Even the doors have ears these days," she muttered as she walked down the hall.

Anne followed meekly. There was no hurrying the Widow now. And there were little buns on the tray. Anne was hungry.

The Widow sat in a large chair near the fireplace and pointed to a settle nearby. Anne sat on the hard-backed bench.

"You say we have four days," the Widow said.

"Oh, no! That was a day and a half ago."

The Widow poured a cup of tea and smiled broadly. "The message will get there and with time to spare, never you fear." She handed the cup to Anne.

Relief flooded Anne. She took the cup and sipped. The warm liquid flowed down her parched throat. She gulped the rest.

The Widow smiled. "You're starving, poor dear. Have a bun."

Anne picked up a bun and took a bite. It was warm and made with real flour. She chewed slowly, savoring the flavor. Mama had used the last of their white flour weeks ago. Now she made only corn bread and oatcakes. There would be no more flour for them until harvest time. And then, unless one of the boys came home to plow and plant, maybe there would be none.

Anne stopped chewing. "Mistress Drew, could I take this home to my mother?"

Tears came to the Widow's eyes and again she blew her nose loudly. "We'll make a bundle of things when I return," she said. "And I'll take you to your mother. Now eat up. And have some more tea."

The Widow moved her chair closer to Anne. "You must promise me to tell no one of what I will now reveal. Do you promise?"

Anne nodded solemnly.

"What I am going to tell you is of the utmost importance. The lives of your brothers, of you and me and your mother, depend on your keeping still in these matters. Do you understand?"

Anne felt her heart quicken and she nodded again.

"Good. You must know that I am putting all our lives in jeopardy, but I have no choice. There is no one else right now." She sighed. "Here's my plan."

Anne leaned over in excitement.

"The roads to the north are watched closely now, what with all the deserters coming and going." She leaned over and whispered, "The general's in the hills, across the Raritan River." She pointed over her shoulder with her thumb.

Anne's eyes widened. "Really? So close?"

The Widow nodded, "Malcolm told me."

"Malcolm? But I thought....," Anne said.

The Widow continued, "He carries news from Congress to the Colonies, so he knows. He sneaked into town the other night and told me about the general." She pulled out her handkerchief and blew her nose. "He looked so pale."

Anne squirmed.

The Widow stuffed her handkerchief into her sleeve and straightened up. "Enough of that. The general's smart to be in the hills, you know. It's easier to protect his men that way. Malcolm told me so. He said the British like to fight out on the open plain. They may be better soldiers but that don't mean they're smarter."

Anne nodded.

"Now," the Widow said, "you just give me the message and I'll see that the general gets it."

"No!" Anne cried. "I've got to go too. I promised. And besides I'm the one who can show the stitchery. I'm the one who did it."

The Widow put down her cup and looked away. She then looked back at Anne and studied her. "You are determined. You know the danger and yet you are determined."

"I am," Anne said. "You must let me go with you."

The Widow sighed, frowned, and then looked up brightly. "I swear, I do have an idea of how to get us out of town. We'll take my carriage. It's over in Culper's shed. I'll bundle you up. We'll tell them you've got the pox and I have to get you out of town. They'll let us go, never fear." She laughed and tapped her head with her finger. "We'll take the ferry across the river and outfox those lobsterbacks."

Anne laughed at the clever scheme. No one would stop them and chance the pox. "I left a note for Mama saying I'd be home tomorrow eve."

The Widow frowned and bit her lip. "We'll be out and back before morning." She got up and scurried to the door. "I'll just pack some things for us to take. A bite to eat. You never know when..."

A loud banging at the door interrupted her. Anne sucked in her breath. The Widow put her finger to her lips. She tiptoed over to the clothes press and opened the heavy door. She motioned for Anne to come. Anne tiptoed over and the Widow pushed her inside. Cloaks and dresses smelling faintly of lavender and thyme smothered Anne. The Widow closed the door.

Moments passed and Anne hardly dared to breathe. She could hear muffled voices but couldn't understand what they were saying. Suddenly the door opened. "Sh-h-h," the Widow whispered. "Don't make a sound." She began to move the dresses as though looking for something. "I'm being taken in to answer some questions regarding Malcolm's whereabouts. Someone has been talking. They think Malcolm's a spy. I may not be long but..."

"The message," Anne whispered.

"Sh-h-h, child." She leaned over and looked deeply into Anne's eyes. "Oh, Annie girl, do be careful. Enemies are everywhere."

"Mistress Drew!" a deep voice bellowed.

"I'm coming, I'm coming," she called. "I can't find my shawl." She reached out and touched Anne's face. "The farrier. You know, Mr. McHugh, the blacksmith. He might help. God bless you, child." She took a dark cloak and then closed the door. Anne heard her footsteps fade away.

Anne waited for what seemed like ages. She felt smothered in the heavy fabrics. Finally, she opened the door of the clothes press. The room was deserted. She hurried to the window and peeked out. No one was in sight. She peeked into the great room and saw that it was empty. Anne walked back to the table and stared at the uneaten buns on the tray. She felt cold all over. Who could go now? Someone had to find the camp and help her deliver the message.

She thought of Ben. If only he were here to help. He'd know what to do. But Ben wasn't here. No one was. The Widow had said that enemies were everywhere. All of the excitement she'd felt a few moments ago was gone. She put her hand in her pocket and felt the stitchery. The message was still safe. She took a deep breath and stood as tall as she could. "I'll see that the general gets it," she said aloud. *The farrier*, she thought. His blacksmith shop was not far off. She'd find him. The Widow said he would help. She picked up her shawl and took the unfinished bun and put it in her other pocket. Quietly she went to the door and opened it. The street was empty. She took a deep breath, stepped outside, and closed the door behind her.

8
Ruffians

The door closed behind Anne with a dull thud and she felt her heart skip a beat. There was no turning back now. *I'll act like nothing is wrong,* she thought. That way no one would be suspicious. She turned to her left and started walking.

Mr. McHugh, the farrier, lived down the street. His blacksmith shop was next to his house. Anne had been there once with Ben to have the horse shod.

A clap of thunder startled her and she ran. In a few moments she reached the shop. No one was there. The fire looked cold. She ran to the house and pounded on the door. "Mistress McHugh," she called and pounded again.

The door opened a crack and Mistress McHugh peeked out. Her eyes were red and swollen and she held a handkerchief to her nose. A little red-haired boy clutched her skirts, smiling shyly at Anne.

"Oh, Anne, it's you. Hurry home, dear. The grenadiers are taking everyone in. They've hired some ruffians—dragged poor John off not two hours ago." She sniffled.

"Gone!" Anne cried. "He can't be."

Mistress McHugh wiped her eyes. "Oh, he's gone all right. Heaven knows when he'll return." She paused. "If..." Then she wiped her eyes again. "Anne, go home to your mother and open the door to no one." She pulled the door to close it.

Anne thrust her foot in the door. "Oh, Mistress McHugh, you must help me. Please."

A baby cried inside the house. Mistress McHugh shook her head. "I can't even help myself. Go home, child. New Brunswick is no longer safe for the likes of us." She pushed Anne's foot out with her own and closed the door.

Anne stood motionless. Her mind was blank. What could she do? She had to think.

She sat down on the stoop and pulled the bun from her pocket. The smell of yeast made her mouth water and she took a big bite. She chewed slowly and noticed that the sun was still above the treetops. The Widow had said the general was in the hills. They weren't *that* far away. If she hurried, she could get to the camp and still be home tomorrow night. There were still two full days before... Her breath caught in her throat and a cold feeling came into her chest. In two days the British troops would be moving toward them. It had been hard enough with the few British soldiers that were quartered in town. Now with troops and the war so close it would be impossible. She scrambled to her feet. She'd eat as she walked.

The bun tasted sweet and she savored it. She hadn't had anything sweet in ever so long. Papa used to bring her sweet candies from town. *Little suckets*, he had called them. That seemed so long ago. She swallowed and took a deep breath. The general was on the other side of the river Raritan. She'd never been across the river before. A new feeling of excitement flushed through her. She took another big bite and stuffed the rest of the bun in her other pocket. She checked to make sure her sewing pouch was still attached to her apron. She thought of her stitchery and felt deep in her pocket. It was there, the French knots like little currants in the fabric. She fingered the chestnut, so smooth in her pocket, and thought of Morgan. An ache formed in her chest. She shook her head. *Oh, I can't think about him now. I've important things to attend to.* She stuffed the corners of her shawl into her waistband and began to run.

It was hard going over the cobblestones, but she kept it up. Suddenly the sun seemed to disappear. She looked up and saw the sky dark with heavy gray clouds. "Please don't rain," she pleaded under her breath.

The street ended abruptly into the main thorough-fare ahead. She turned the corner and ran right into a mob of boys. A rough hand grabbed her arm and swung her about. "Hoy, lads, what have we here?"

Anne looked up into an unshaven face and pulled back. The man leaned close to her. His breath smelled foully of rum. "Why, it's a wench," he bellowed. He grabbed her waist and picked her up and held her high in the air. "Maybe we should take *her* in for questioning."

Anne felt a rush of cool air on her legs and saw her skirts swirl out over the heads of the small boys. She felt her face and neck flame hot in embarrassment.

The crowd roared with laughter.

Anne kicked the man and then kicked again. Slowly, he lowered her, and the boys crowded closely around. Anne looked about wildly. A feeling of panic gripped her chest.

"Let me go, please," she begged.

"Oh," he mimicked in a high falsetto. "Let me go. Oh, please, *sir*."

Tears smarted Anne's eyes. "You brute," she spit out the words as she tried to strike him. "Let me go!"

The man threw back his head and laughed. "Brute, am I?" His fingers tightened into Anne's arms. "Well, we'll..."

A horse came racing around the corner and reared, frightened by the crowd. The boys scattered and the man pulled Anne against the building.

With her free hand, she reached for her pouch and began to work her fingers inside.

"Out of my way!" the rider shouted as he struggled to get his horse back under control. He waved his fist at the man and then raced away.

The brute waved his fist back at the rider.

Anne finally found the tiny scissors. Quickly she pulled them out and thrust them into the man's arm.

"Ow!" he bellowed and let go. Anne pulled away. "Why, you..."

He grabbed her shoulder and pulled her back. Anne screamed. Just then, a group of older boys came running around the corner. Morgan Jones was with them, his black hair plastered against his pale cheeks. "Anne!" The word exploded from his lips. "It's Anne..."

"Ah," the brute said. "Ye know her."

"She's Anne...uh-h, my sister," he blurted and he rushed to Anne's side. He grabbed her arm. "Come on. I'll take you home."

The man pushed Anne toward Morgan. "Oh, the devil take ye both." He turned. "Where are me lads?" he called. "We've yet another house to find." He stumbled down the street and the boys followed, taunting him, pushing and shoving.

Morgan put his arm around Anne and hurried her away. "What are you doing here?" he asked. He looked back over his shoulder and hurried Anne along.

When they reached the end of the street, Morgan finally stopped. "You shouldn't be here, Anne. It's not safe."

"You helped me," she said softly.

His face colored. "I couldn't let him hurt you. Why are you here?"

Anne wanted desperately to tell him about the soldier, about "Griffin" and the code but she dared not. Morgan's father was a Tory, sworn to defend the King. They'd arrest her and hang her for a spy. Her mouth went dry at the thought.

"Anne," Morgan asked again, "why are you here?"

She had to tell him something. "The Widow Drew."

Morgan frowned. "Yes?"

"I brought her a decoction Mama made and some burnt alum for her misery."

"Oh."

"You saved me," Anne said and her voice broke.

Morgan patted her back. "Don't cry, Anne, please don't."

Anne straightened. "I am not crying. I'm just grateful is all."

Again, Morgan's face turned bright pink. "I'm sorry about what's happened. You know...that last time...when my father and your father. Well, when my father said those terrible things to your father. He was just so fired up. Maybe he didn't mean it."

"Oh, he meant it all right," Anne said.

"It doesn't seem proper," Morgan said softly. "All this arguing and fighting in families." He paused and the muscles in his jaw moved. "I mean with your family and Faith's acting like they are enemies. I just wish we could all be friends again. You know, like we were."

Anne felt her heart swell as Morgan looked at her. His eyes looked black against his milky skin. A faint shadow of mustache showed on his upper lip.

They heard a shout in the distance. Morgan stepped closer. "We have to get you out of here." He put his arm about her waist.

Anne felt her breath quicken. "Take me to the Widow's."

As she walked beside Morgan, she could feel the warmth of his body. He seemed so strong, and taller somehow. Her heart made little fluttering movements. When they reached the Widow's house they stopped, but he didn't lower his arm. "Anne."

She looked into his face. "Yes?"

He took a deep breath. "My family is going back to England."

"England!"

"Yes," he hurried on. "My father said we belong there. We're British subjects. Faith's family is going too. Couldn't you go with them?"

Anne shook her head.

Morgan looked down. "No, I suppose not what with your family being Whigs and all." They were silent.

Then Morgan spoke. "Remember the day when Hamish threw the mud at your mother?"

Anne nodded. She would never forget that day.

Morgan's face colored. "That was a low thing to do. I'm ashamed I was there." He paused and looked away. "I don't know much about what's happening now. I'm not like Adam. But I'm not like Ben either. I'm sort of in the middle." He looked at Anne. "You're a Rebel, aren't you, Anne?"

Anne's voice was soft. "Yes, and proud to be so."

Morgan nodded. "I don't know what I am." He sighed. "I don't know what I'll do in England. Perhaps I'll study for the law, or a trade."

Anne felt tears crowd her eyes. "This is a wondrous land. Papa always said so."

Morgan sighed. "I'm sure that it is." He looked at Anne. "Faith and I will miss you."

Her heart stopped. "Faith?"

"Yes. We often speak of you, of the good times we had before." He paused. "You know, before the troubles began."

Anne felt as though the blood had drained from her face.

Morgan squeezed her shoulder. "I will miss you."

Tears choked Anne's throat and she tried to swallow.

"If I write, will you write back?" he asked.

She nodded.

"I'll tell Faith to write too."

His eyes seemed to look right through her. Quickly, he kissed her cheek. He held her a moment longer, then he let her go and ran down the street. At the corner he stopped and waved. Anne waved back. Then he turned the corner and was gone.

Anne held her breath, trying to engrave his image in her mind. She turned and opened the Widow's bright blue door and stepped inside. She heard the lock catch as the door closed behind her. Slowly she slumped to the floor.

Her heart was pounding and her face was wet with perspiration and tears. She picked up a corner of her apron to wipe her face and saw she was still clutching the scissors. She shuddered at the sight of the blood smeared on the blades. The memory of the man's rough hands on her filled her with dread. Then she thought of the warmth of Morgan's hand and his dark eyes. She touched her cheek as she thought of his kiss. Tears formed and she tried to gulp them back but couldn't.

She sighed. He would be in England and Faith would win his heart. She leaned against the door and let the tears spill down her cheeks.

9
The River Raritan

A loud clap of thunder woke Anne. She jumped up and looked about. The room was dark and the fire nearly out. It took a few moments for Anne to figure out where she was. Then she remembered. She was at the Widow Drew's and Morgan was gone. Her heart sank. Morgan was going to England. She would never see him again. Not ever.

She reached into her pocket for her handkerchief and brought out her stitchery. It was still there, still undelivered. Oh why had she ever promised she would take it! It had seemed such a simple thing to do at the time. Back then it seemed that all she had to do was get it to New Brunswick. Now she was left to carry the message alone. *Mama will be furious with me,* she thought. *She'll probably never forgive me.*

Anne sighed. But if she hadn't come, she would never have seen Morgan. Never had felt his kiss. Never have known of his leaving. She would have continued in her daydreams. But no longer. She must put thoughts of Morgan out of her head forever. She sighed. She had given her word that the message would be delivered. She would keep that promise.

Rain pounding against the glass broke the quiet. Anne looked out and wondered how long she had dallied. Sheets of water were pouring down. *Oh no,* she thought. *I should never have talked with Morgan for so long.* She thought again of being with him, and felt a pain near her heart.

A sigh escaped her. Crying over spilt milk wouldn't help anything. Mama always said that. Anne had vowed to grow up and be dependable. This was truly her chance to do so. She straightened her cap and tucked a strand of hair back inside. Carefully, she folded the stitchery and put it back into her pocket. What would Morgan think if he knew what she was doing? She shook her head. It was best not to have such thoughts.

"I'd best be on my way," she said aloud. She had to get to the camp. Only two days before the troops would be outside the town. She had to try again. Only this time she'd stay off the busy streets.

Just as suddenly as it started, the rain stopped. Anne looked out the window. The wet street glistened in the evening light, and little rivulets of water ran between the stones.

No one was in sight. Little wonder. The town had been taken over by ruffians. She smoothed down her dress and rinsed her hands and face. Amongst the dishes on the table she saw a heel of bread and stuffed it in her pocket. The Widow wouldn't mind. Anne was sure of that.

The street was clear when she opened the door. The evening air smelled clean and wet. She closed the door behind her and hurried to the corner. Slowly, she peeked around the rough brick wall. No more running foolishly into mobs. She tucked in her shawl, straightened her cap, and walked briskly down the street. She'd get to the river, but she'd go the long way. She felt drained, empty. *Maybe I'll see Ben in the camp,* she thought, and felt her spirits rise.

Block by block she made her way, avoiding any streets with people. Pale lights shone through the windows. Anne thought of her mother and of home. She wondered how the soldier was and what Mama was doing. Maybe she'd made a custard with the milk and eggs. Anne's stomach rumbled and she pulled the heel of bread from her pocket. She munched slowly, making the taste last as long as she could.

A pale moon was trying to show through the straggling clouds. Suddenly, she saw the river, dark and angry looking. She found the path easily and followed it to the riverbank. Anne stared at the turbulent water. She'd never seen water like this before. It was pounding and crashing against the bank.

On the opposite side were the hills. She could see thin trails of smoke from campfires. *That's where the camp is,* she thought. She was almost there. She smiled. What would Ben think when he saw his baby sister bringing a message about the British generals. He'd be so proud.

The path along the river was wide and she walked quickly. The ferry had to be nearby. Suddenly, her legs hit a rope and she nearly tipped over. She grabbed a nearby tree to stop her fall. *What is that doing here,* she wondered, *stretched across the path like this?* The rope disappeared into the bushes beside the river. She lifted her skirts and stepped over it.

"Hey, Jock," a voice called out.

Anne ducked behind the tree.

"Who goes?" a man's voice answered.

Anne peeked out. There was the ferry. Clearly, she could see the barge in the water. The door to the ferryman's cabin was open and pale yellow light formed a pattern on the wooden dock and the choppy water beyond.

"I've come to relieve you," the voice called again. "And I've brought a grenadier with me."

Anne squinted her eyes and stared. There on the dock were two men, the night ferryman and a British soldier. Anne leaned her head against the tree. What could she do now? She had to get across that river. It felt as if her very life were draining out of her.

"I think the storm's passed," the soldier said.

"Looks that way," the day ferryman answered. "Are you staying?"

"Aye," the soldier answered. "There'll be no Rebels crossing at this spot, I warrant. There were campfires in the hills last night. We're taking no chances."

"Well, I'm off," said the day ferryman. "Them Rebels will turn tail when they see that red coat of your'n."

The soldier laughed. "They'll get their fill, I'll warrant."

Anne watched as the day ferryman walked up to the road and headed for town. The night ferryman walked to the edge of the dock and studied the river.

"Water's high," he said.

They then entered the small cabin and closed the door.

Anne sneaked closer. The barge looked huge in the dark water. She could never work it alone. Her shoulders drooped as did her spirits. She couldn't stop now. She was so close. There had to be another way. She turned around and retraced her steps.

When she reached the rope she climbed over it again. Curious, she followed the rope into the bushes. Something dark was floating in the water. What could it be? Anne slid down the bank. She sucked in her breath. There was a rowboat. That could get her across the river! She untied the heavy rope and climbed in. Two inches of water sloshed over her boots, soaking the hem of her dress. Two oars were resting in the oarlocks. She felt herself get warm with excitement. She'd never rowed a boat, but she'd seen pictures of oarsmen in boats. It couldn't be too hard.

Anne picked up one of the oars and pushed away from the bank. The boat moved slightly. She could do it! Her heart soared. With all her strength, she pushed again, and the boat floated into the river. She was going to make it.

The oar slid easily into its lock and Anne sat down. *Here we go*, she thought, and lowered the handles. She moved her arms forward, dropped the oars into the water and pulled. The boat glided across the water. She wanted to shout she was so happy. She pulled again on the oars. This time they lifted out of the water and she fell over backwards. The bow of the boat lifted, then splashed loudly back into the water. Maybe this wasn't going to be so easy after all.

Stroke by stroke, Anne pulled the oars. She had spotted a tree on the farther bank. *I'll use it as a guide*, she thought. But the current was swift and she began to drift down toward the ferry. Again, the oars skimmed the water and splashed loudly.

"Ahoy, there!"

Anne looked up. The soldier had stepped outside of the cabin and was peering in her direction. She crouched low in the boat and waited.

"Who goes there?" the soldier called. "There's a boat adrift," he called over his shoulder.

The ferryman answered from inside the cabin. "Probably old Andrew's. He's always forgetting to tie it up. It drifts down there most every night. Hey, there's a draft. Get in here and close that door."

Anne listened until she heard the cabin door close, then she peeked over the edge of the boat. The soldier had gone inside. She sat up and looked about. The boat had drifted even further. It would take some heavy pulling to get across.

A breeze came up and Anne felt goose pimples rise on her arms. She tied her shawl tighter about her shoulders and then bent again to her task. Her hands began to burn and her arms ached, but she kept pulling. The moon had again gone behind a cloud and Anne couldn't see the far bank. She stopped to rest and arched her back. Even hoeing had never been this hard. She held her sore palms and then put them in the cold water. That eased the hurt only a little. Maybe some padding would help. Anne took her skirt and wrapped it around the oar handles. She then went back to pulling the oars. She was drifting more rapidly now. She counted the pulls, hoping it would help. One...two...three...It didn't. The rowing was getting harder. Then she tried to remember some of the pieces she'd memorized with Faith.

She was afraid of being heard, and so she whispered, a line for each pull of the oars.

"O Love, they wrong thee much

That say thy sweet is bitter,"

She frowned, trying to remember the next lines. She couldn't. "Dada dada dada," she said, keeping the meter going. "Dada dada dada." The oars skimmed the water and she fell backwards. She righted herself and continued trying to remember the poem. She and Faith had found it among Aunt Elizabeth's things. What were those lines? "Dada dada dada," she whispered, and then smiled. She could remember the rest.

"where truest pleasure is,
I do adore thee;
I know thee what thou art,
I serve thee with my heart,
And fall before thee."

She thought of Morgan. Little did she dream when she and Faith had giggled over the lines that someday she would understand them. Could she say, "I do adore thee?" She blushed at the thought. How would she feel when he was oceans away and she might never see him again? Tears filled her eyes.

The boat hit the shore with a soft thud and Anne tumbled over backwards. Quickly she got up and grabbed at a bush and pulled the boat in as far as she could. The rope was wet, but she grabbed it and climbed out. Then she tied the boat to a shrub. Her wet skirts clung to her legs. She wrung them out and noticed that her hands were blistered and throbbing. She was wet and cold, but she had crossed the river Raritan alone.

Clouds had again darkened the skies and she couldn't see the ferry house. Gentle hills rolled away before her. She'd follow them until she saw the campfires. The British grenadiers were only two days away. There was still plenty of time to deliver the message and hurry home to Mama. She found a path and struck out toward the hills.

10

Captured

Moonlight again flooded the path, and Anne walked quickly. She had gone only a few yards when she noticed a man ahead of her carrying a musket. His clothes were a dark drab olive, not red, and he wore a strange looking hat. He was looking beyond the hills, his musket cradled in his arms. She looked carefully at his countenance. He was clean shaven, seemed rather young, and was almost handsome. *He must be a Rebel soldier,* she thought, and she quickened her pace.

What a relief, Anne thought. At last she could deliver the message and then go home. She felt light-headed with hunger and fatigue. Maybe they'd even feed her and give her some hot tea. Her mouth watered at the thought. Perhaps they'd have a dry shift she could wear so she could dry her clothes. Oh, it would be so wonderful. And they could row her back across the river.

The man ahead turned and saw her. He raised his musket. "Halt!"

Anne stepped forward. "Oh, sir, it's only me and I've a message for the general."

The man lowered his musket and stepped forward. "*Fräulein?*" he questioned.

Anne frowned.

He spoke more strange words that Anne had never heard before. Who was he? She turned cold all over. Maybe he wasn't a soldier. All the whispers she'd heard about what happened to young girls found wandering in the woods came crowding back. Terror gripped Anne's chest. "You're not a Rebel soldier," she cried and she turned and began to run.

The man was right behind her and quickly caught her.

"*Fräulein*," he said. "*Komm.*" He pulled her arm and said something in his foreign tongue.

"Let me go!" Anne said and tried to jerk her arm away. He shrugged and then started walking, dragging Anne along with him.

Anne twisted and turned trying to get away, but he held her fast. She kicked at his legs, and he laughed and then twisted her arm behind her back. She cried out in pain. He pushed her out in front and nudged her back with his knee. Her heart beat wildly, and her arm stung with pain, so she walked quietly.

They soon approached a few tents. Small fires ringed with men dressed in the drab uniforms were scattered about. The man called out in his strange language. The others looked up and laughed. Several of the men came over to more closely inspect Anne. One young man grabbed her chin to turn her face toward him. He smelled of smoke and sweat. At his touch Anne swung out with her free hand and slapped his face. "Don't you dare touch me, you brute!"

The men roared with laughter. From one of the larger tents, a man emerged. He was dressed in the familiar red uniform of the British grenadiers. When he saw Anne, he hurried over and spoke in the strange language. The men went back to their fires.

The man holding Anne let her go, and he too went away. Anne rubbed her aching arm. "Well, miss," the officer said. "Who are you? And what are you doing out alone at this hour?"

Anne clenched her jaw. She would have nothing to do with this Britisher. She turned her head away from the man.

"Speak up, girl." His voice had a hard edge to it. "I haven't time for any nonsense. Have you come looking for someone?"

Anne straightened her back and continued to stare off into the distance.

The officer stepped closer. "Come, child. Who are you? Just tell me and then we can give you safe conduct back home." He tapped his riding crop against his leg. "If it's a young man you're looking for, I can help."

Her mind raced. She had to tell him something. If she told him her real name he might know Papa had been in the Sons of Liberty. He'd think she was a spy and hang her. She gulped.

"Well?" he demanded.

She had to say something. Her eyes widened. She knew what to do. "I'm Faith," she said sweetly. "Faith Sheffield."

The officer pulled out a small, dark notebook from his vest and opened it. "Sheffield, you say."

"Yes. And my father is..."

He interrupted. "Tobias Sheffield."

Anne was surprised. How did he know that?

"And why did you come here, lass?" he peered at her over the notebook.

It felt as if his pale blue eyes could pierce right through her. She had never thought about what to do in a situation like this. In her imagination, she just walked right up to the Rebel camp. Then she imagined the soldiers in their bright blue uniforms had taken her to see general Washington. She would then give them the code and the general would thank her. She would then be given a piece of linen large enough to do a coverlet. Those were the daydreams she had had. She never dreamed anything like this could happen.

"Well, answer me."

"I...I...," Anne stammered.

"You don't have an answer, do you?" he said through a clenched jaw. He grabbed her wrist and shook her. "You aren't Faith Sheffield any more than I am! The Sheffields are on their way to England."

Anne gasped. How did he know that?

"Why did you lie?"

Anne swallowed and tried to pull away. The officer held her even tighter. Anne dug in her heels and struggled to get free. "Let me go," she pleaded. "I've got a message." She sucked in her breath. Why ever had she said that?

The officer let her go. "Did old Andrew send you?"

Anne nodded.

"Well?"

Anne breathed deeply. What could she say? She thought wildly. "Um..."

The officer leaned forward.

Then she got an idea. "The Widow Drew was taken in for questioning," she said.

"Yes, yes. What else?"

"And Mr. McHugh."

"Girl, we know all of that. It was our man who gave us the names." He frowned at her. "You don't have a message, do you?" He put his notebook back into his vest. "So why would you be out here?" he pondered. "A beau perhaps?"

She shook her head. "Oh, no!"

"Then?" he paused. "Are you snooping around? Well, I'll have no spies in this camp." He grabbed her arm and pulled her toward the tent.

Anne screamed. "Help! Somebody please help!"

The flap to the tent opened and a tall dark-haired man stepped out. He frowned and then a look of shock covered his face. "Anne?" he called.

Anne looked up. It couldn't be, but it was. "Ben!" she cried. The officer let her go and she ran and threw herself into the arms of her brother.

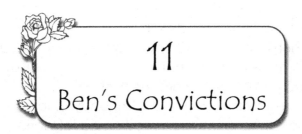

11
Ben's Convictions

"Oh, Ben," Anne cried.

Ben held her close and patted her back. "There, there, Annie, my girl. It's all right." He looked up at the officer. "She's my sister, sir."

"Sister? What a nuisance. Wouldn't even tell me her name."

"Sir, she's just a child and frightened."

"Well, get her out of here. We haven't much time."

"I will, sir. Could she use your tent? To get herself together."

The officer muttered a reply and Ben led Anne into the tent. She felt weak with relief. He led her to a cot and sat her down. "Anne, how did you get here? What are you doing here? Did Uncle Tobias bring you?"

Anne shook her head.

"Where's Mama?" Ben asked.

"Home."

"Home! You mean she let you come alone?"

"She doesn't know."

"Doesn't know!" the cords on Ben's neck bulged. "Anne Elizabeth Brewster! You should be horsewhipped.

Running around the countryside alone. Mama must be sick with worry." He frowned. "Anne, what are you doing here?"

Fear gripped Anne's throat and she made a little strangled sound. "I went to see the Widow," she said. "And then I got lost and that soldier found me and....Oh, Ben, I so hoped I'd find you." She leaned forward and whispered, "Are we prisoners?"

Ben shook his head. "I'll explain it all later. But, why were you looking for me? Is Mama sick?"

Anne shook her head. Tears streamed down her cheeks and she hiccupped a sob.

Ben patted her shoulder. "There, there, don't cry, Annie. You're all right now. I'll take care of you. You're wet through." Ben turned and began rummaging through a trunk. "Whatever am I going to do with you?"

Anne shivered and hiccupped dry little sobs.

"Don't cry. You're safe now." He held up a long white nightshirt. "This will do." He handed it to Anne. "Take off those wet things," Ben said as he turned around. "Go on. You'll take a terrible chill."

Anne pulled off the wet dress and her shift. She pulled the nightshirt over her head. The fabric felt coarse, but it was dry. She slipped off her boots and stockings.

Ben peeked over his shoulder. "Here," he reached for her dress.

Anne thought of the stitchery and a cold feeling went over her heart. *This is a British tent,* she thought, *I'd best be careful.* She clutched her dress. "I'll do it." She shook the dress carefully and then stretched it over the end of the table. She laid her stockings nearby.

Anne reached for the stitchery in her pocket and started to pull it out, but then thought better of it. Best to leave it safe for now. She sat down on the cot.

Ben lit a candle on the table. Anne saw that his face looked older. The brass buttons on his waistcoat glimmered in the pale yellow light. It must be new, she thought. She'd never seen him in a waistcoat like that before. He looked so dignified, like a real gentleman. He sat down on a little canvas-topped stool.

"Now tell me all about it, Anne. How ever did you find me?"

"The boat floated too far, and I couldn't row it. Oh, Ben, I so hoped to find you." A sob caught in her throat. Then her eyes widened and she looked about. "Are we prisoners?" she whispered.

Quickly, Ben stood and walked away. "No." His voice sounded tired somehow.

"But, Ben, they're Britishers, and who are those strange soldiers?"

Ben still didn't face her. "They're mercenaries. German soldiers hired by the British. They're an advance group scouting the area."

"But, Ben, if they're British, and we aren't prisoners..." She didn't finish the sentence. "Ben, I don't understand."

Slowly, Ben spoke. "Because I am one of them."

"You're a soldier?"

Ben shook his head. "No. I supply them with information."

Anne gasped. "You're a spy!"

"Anne, don't be so dramatic. No, I am not a spy. But my office affords me important information, and they pay me well."

"Pay you!" Anne was shocked.

Ben turned to her. "Anne, where do you think the money has come from to buy your supplies? My service to the British has allowed me to take care of you and Mama."

Anne sat stunned, not believing what she'd heard.

Ben came and kneeled before her. He grabbed her hands and held them tight. "Don't you see?" he asked. "It's the only way. The Rebels can never win this war. Not against England. It's the most powerful country in the world. Our future lies with the British."

He got up and began to pace. "In a few months it will all be over. Uncle Tobias is on his way to England and I can have his position. They promised me. Then I can really take care of you and Mama. Adam can have the farm. He's always wanted it. And you and Mama will come into town and live with me."

Anne said nothing. She felt dead inside. Ben had gone over to the British. Her own Ben. She couldn't believe it.

Her voice was quiet when she spoke. "Papa said our cause was just."

"Papa!" Ben spit out the word. "Papa was a hopeless dreamer, surely you see that. Reading his pamphlets and going to secret meetings. What did it bring us? Isolation, grief, death. And poor Mama."

An aide entered the tent with a tray. "Tea," he said. He placed the tray on the table and left.

Ben took a large steaming mug of tea and gave it to Anne. "Here, you look as though you could use this."

Anne took the mug mechanically and took a sip. The tea was strong and hot and she sipped slowly. Was this really Ben talking like this? She glanced at him over the rim of the mug and remembered his last few months at home. Had he changed? Was this the same Ben she had so loved when she was little?

"We're English, Anne. British subjects. Our future lies with them."

"What about Adam?" Anne whispered.

Ben shook his head. "Stubborn young fool. Just like Papa. I tried reasoning with him but to no avail. I hope to God he comes out of this alive." He took the mug from Anne and placed it on the table. "You look exhausted. Here, lie down." She lowered her head to the hard pillow. "Rest. I'll be back."

Anne raised her head. "But Ben..."

"Don't fret. You'll be safe here." He covered her with a blanket. Then he left the tent.

What would she do? Anne got up and felt in the pocket of her dress for the stitchery. It was still there. Damp, but safe. She lay down and closed her eyes but she couldn't sleep. Her mind was racing with thoughts. How could Ben have become a Loyalist? They had grown up in the same house together. They had listened to all of Papa's arguments. Surely Ben knew that the King was being unfair. He must know the Colonies needed to govern themselves. Even she understood that.

The change had come to Ben after he'd started working for Uncle Tobias. He had been delighted with his new work and stayed in town during the week. He had only come to the farm when he was needed. Ben was so different from Adam. Ben liked being in town. He liked wearing nice waistcoats and fine shirts. She felt a lump in her throat. But that didn't mean he had to become a Tory. Lots of Whigs wore fine waistcoats and silk shirts. *Oh, what would Papa think?*

She wondered again what she should do. If she didn't take the message, Adam might be killed. If she did, then Ben might die. Her head ached with her thinking. How could she choose? What should she do?

Exhaustion washed over her and she closed her eyes. She had to think of something, she just had to. Slowly, she drifted into sleep.

Ben shook her gently. She sat up and moaned. She ached all over.

"Anne," Ben said softly. "I'll take you home, but I can't until later. There's something I have to do right now. The mercenaries are moving out shortly. But, they'll leave this tent and a couple of guards. No one will bother you now. I've seen to that."

Anne felt as if she was made of wood. Dear kind Ben talking like a stranger.

Ben studied her face. "You look exhausted."

"Brewster!" a voice called. Anne recognized the voice of the British officer.

"I must be off." Ben reached over and kissed Anne's forehead. "I'm a Brewster, just like you and Adam. And we Brewsters must live by our convictions. I hope that some day you'll understand." He walked over to the small table and picked up some papers. He folded them and tucked them into a pocket in his waistcoat. Then he kissed her forehead again. "Get some rest. I'll soon be back and take you home to Mama." He put his hat on. "I have work to do. I'll be back in a few hours." He tucked the blanket around her legs. "You should never have left home." Ben turned and left the tent.

Anne sat frozen, staring at the swinging tent flap. Tears filled her eyes. How could Ben talk like that? Anne longed to grab him and hold him. If only she could undo all of this. If only she could get life back to the way it used to be. Papa had died for his convictions. Would Ben or Adam have to die for theirs? She dropped onto the hard pillow and sobbed.

12
Anne's Decision

The tent began to glow with the pale yellow light of morning. Anne realized she was staring, not thinking, not feeling, just being numb. So much had happened. She sighed. It would soon be day. She wondered where Ben had gone and when he'd be back.

The mugs of tea were still on the table. She jumped up and drank, emptying her mug. It was cold, but real English tea. She hadn't had any for ever so long. Then she emptied the other. Her cheeks burned with shame. What would Papa say? She put the mug down quickly. There were some seed cakes on the tray. She was famished. She picked one up and bit into it.

She could hear voices speaking that strange language. She peeked outside. The men were dismantling the tents.

Her dress was still on the table. It felt almost dry. There was a large tear in the skirt, and a seam in the bodice had been pulled open. She sighed. It had been a good dress, her favorite shade of pale green. She had worn it on their last picnic—she, Faith, and Morgan.

Even if she mended it carefully, it would never be the same. And then she thought of the stitchery.

Anne went back to the cot and plunked herself down. What was she going to do? She'd promised the wounded soldier that the message would be delivered to General Washington.

She ached all over. She looked at her hands. Her palms were covered with blisters, one beginning to look red and angry. How had she missed the Rebel camp? She'd been told the Rebel soldiers were in the hills above the Raritan. Then she remembered. She'd floated down the river quite a distance. She must have missed the landing for the Rebel camp. No doubt if she followed the river back, she'd find it.

A feeling of excitement ran through her. Then she thought about Ben. Anne shook her head. If only it were more simple. If someone would only tell her what was right. But there was no one here who could do that. She had to decide for herself.

She climbed back under the blanket and bundled up. She had vowed that she would grow up and be dependable, not be a spoiled child anymore. And now was the time to think about that clearly. What to do would be her decision, hers alone. How did she feel about the war? Whose side would she choose? She frowned. That was the question that Morgan had to think about as well. This business of being grown up was not going to be easy.

She thought of the young soldier at home with Mama. War was a terrible thing, and she didn't want anyone hurt. Then she remembered the words Thomas Paine had written. He said that the cause of America is the cause of all mankind. Anne bit her lower lip as she pondered just what that could mean. It had something to do with being governed by someone who just took power away from you. Someone who wouldn't let you represent yourself in his government. The King and his Parliament were treating the Americans as if they were just children. There were some good things about having a strong parent. Papa had been one, but he had always listened to her and entertained her ideas. *What would it be like to continue with the King?* she wondered.

She tried to see herself a Loyalist like Faith and Ben. She could live with Ben and he'd take care of her. *But living isn't just about being taken care of,* she thought. She wanted to grow up and take care of herself. Hadn't she gotten here all by herself? *And what about our rights?* she wondered. The Colonies had grown up and now could take care of themselves. They had tried every way possible to get the King and his Parliament to listen to their complaints. But to no avail. The King still acted like a benevolent father, and he made them pay dearly for that. "It's abuse," Papa would say, and then would quote from the Declaration of Independence. Over and over he had quoted those phrases. She couldn't remember exactly, but it was something about when a long train of abuses and usurpations had gone on, it was the right—no, the duty—to throw off such a Government.

Did she really believe that? She looked to see how she felt. *Am I a Loyalist?* From deep inside, the word *No!* rose. *I'm a Rebel,* she thought, and was surprised how true that felt. *I'm a Rebel, and not because Papa says so, or Adam. I say so. And a Brewster must live her convictions.*

A tiny spot of fear started in her chest. If the British found out, who knew what they would do? She shivered at the thought. But she could not—would not—deny who she was. *I'll just be careful*, she thought. She wondered what Ben would think when she was gone. Tears filled her eyes. She hoped he wouldn't hate her.

Quickly, she tossed the blanket aside and got up. She had to get out of here. She peeked outside. Only one soldier was visible near the fire. Everyone else was gone. Ben said they were moving out.

She pulled on her stockings, still clammy cold. Then she pulled off the warm nightshirt and laid it over the cot. Goose pimples popped out on her arms. Her shift was damp as she pulled it over her head, and she shivered. She pulled on her dress, also damp and cold. Her shawl was missing. Probably lost someplace. She'd have to do without. Her stomach rumbled with hunger. She looked at the tray. Seed cakes would have to do. The remains of the bread and buns were a gooey mess in her pocket. She stuffed the little cakes down on top.

Anne peeked out of the tent. A thin line of smoke drifted up from the fire. The soldier was hunkered down, lifting a large pot from the coals. His back was to her. She looked about. No one else was in sight. Quickly, she stepped outside. There was the opening in the woods with the path back to the river.

The soldier looked up. "*Fräulein!*"

Anne froze.

"*Fräulein*, your brother come tonight."

"Thank you."

"I make you tea?"

"Yes, please." She stepped back into the tent and peeked out. The soldier went back to his work at the fire.

Anne went to the back of the tent, grabbed the heavy canvas, and pulled as hard as she could. Nothing gave. She sighed. She'd have to crawl under. She dropped to her knees and wormed her way under the tent. The ground was soft and stained her dress. No time to worry about that. She looked about. No one was in sight. Quickly she stood and started running. She didn't stop until she was on the path.

As she neared the river, she slowed, looking and listening for the sentry. He was nearby, she was sure, for she could smell his pipe. She crouched behind a tree and peeked out toward the river. There he was, sitting on the bank, blowing smoke rings into the air. The boat was gone. But she had no need for it. She walked carefully through the woods around the sentry until she was sure he could not see her. Then she stepped onto the path and began to run. With each step, she remembered her loss of Ben and her heart ached. It was as if he had died.

13
The Rebel Camp

The path along the river was easy to follow in the early dawn light. She ran until she saw the gentle, rolling hills. The camp was back in there. The grenadiers hoped the Rebels would come out into the valley where they'd be easy targets. She was glad the Rebels had stayed in the hills, safe from the British guns.

She felt winded, but continued walking as fast as she could. The running had warmed her. With each step she thought of the magic word—"Griffin."

Soon, pale columns of smoke rose not far off. She wanted to shout with joy. Then she sobered. This time she'd make sure it was the right camp. She slowed her walk and began searching the horizon for some sign.

A young man came over the rise of the hill ahead. He stopped, raised his musket, and looked Anne up and down. Then he lowered his musket and smiled.

Anne stared. His clothes were shabby and worn.

"Miss," he called. "Where are you going all alone?"

"I'm looking for the Rebel camp," she called out.

The young man approached. "What need have you of the camp? Have you brought us clean linen?"

He smiled shyly. "Or have you come to see a brother? Or a young man? We have lots of young ladies coming by with messages for husbands and brothers. By the way, where do you hail from?"

She tilted her head toward the river. "New Brunswick."

"Lots of Loyalists there, I hear."

Anne nodded.

"But there are some fine lads from this area with us."

"I need to see someone in the camp. I have a message for him."

"I can take it for you."

"No! I must deliver it in person. I promised."

The soldier studied Anne and then frowned. "How did you find this place?"

"The Widow Drew told me."

"Ah, yes, the Widow. Well, come along then."

He turned and started back up the hill.

Anne walked briskly. *Soon there*, she thought. At long last.

They arrived at the crest of the hill, and there was the camp spread out before her. There were tents with small fires and men making tea and talking together. Anne was shocked. They looked so shabby. Not in fine blue uniforms at all.

"There you are, miss." He pointed. "The officers' tent has the flags in front. Ask for the Officer of the Day. He can help you find your young man."

Anne smiled with relief. "Thank you."

The soldier nodded and returned to his post.

Anne walked toward the camp. Maybe Adam was here. A soldier approached shyly. "Looking for someone, miss?" he asked.

She nodded. "Yes, General Washington."

"Well, miss..." The soldier hesitated.

"Anne! Anne Elizabeth!"

Anne turned toward the voice. There, standing by a campfire was Adam. His clothes were worn and soiled, his legs bare. A scruffy beard showed on his pale cheeks, and his eyes blazed bright blue.

"Adam!" Anne shouted.

"Annie!" He ran to her and scooped her up. Then he frowned. "What in blazes are you doing here?"

"Adam, your clothes...where are your stockings?"

"Anne, how did you get here? Is Mama sick?"

Anne straightened as tall as she could. "I've got a message for General Washington."

The men sitting about the fire smiled and Adam whooped. "Surely you do! You said you'd get into this man's army somehow, but a message! And for the general!" He bent over with laughter.

Anne's face flushed hot in embarrassment and anger. "I do so. I found a wounded man and he said he had a message for the general and he gave it to me and it's in code and I know the code."

"Oh, Annie!" He took her arm and started to lead her away. "I don't know how you ever got here, but you must get home. This is no place..."

Anne pulled away from him. "Adam, I nearly got myself killed getting here. You'd best listen to me. You hear?"

Adam smiled and took her arm again. "Anne. Anne. Quiet down. You're being a downright nuisance. I'll have to get leave to take you home. You wait here. My mates will take care of you, won't you, lads?"

The men nodded their agreement.

Anne looked about. Brightly colored flags were flying above the tent before them. She noticed it was larger than the others. *This must be the officers' tent,* she thought. Anne pulled her arm away from Adam and darted into the tent. She tripped over a small rug and sprawled before the surprised officers.

Adam burst into the tent. "Oh, sirs, I'm so sorry. It's my little sister. I'll send her back home."

The men laughed politely.

An officer stood. "You do that, Brewster."

Adam grabbed Anne's arm and pulled her to her feet. "Sorry for the inconvenience," he said as he dragged Anne out of the tent.

"Now you've gone and done it," Adam said. He marched angrily toward his tent, dragging Anne along behind him.

14
The General

Adam pulled Anne along. "Oh, Anne, how embarrassing. What ever will I do with you?"

Anne stopped and stared at Adam, her jaw set firmly. "Adam Brewster. You think you're so...so..." She shook her head, so angry she could hardly speak. "Well," she said, "I do have a message and not you nor anyone else is going to stop me." She turned quickly and ran back into the tent.

The officers looked up, surprised.

"Griffin!" Anne shouted.

The men looked startled.

Adam dashed in and grabbed Anne's arm. "Sirs," he said. "I'm..."

"Quiet," the officer said. He came around the table and stood before Anne. "What did you say?" he asked.

"Griffin," she answered timidly.

The man looked back at the other officers and then again at Anne. "And where did you hear this word, miss?"

Adam stood, open-mouthed.

Anne took a deep breath. "I found a wounded man. He's in my home right now and Mama is caring for him. He's badly hurt."

"Yes," the man said impatiently.

"Get on with it," Adam whispered.

"Well, he said he had a message for General Washington and would I take it. I promised I would."

"And the message?" the officer prompted.

Anne brought out the soggy stitchery and spread it on the table. The men looked at it and then at Anne.

She smiled. It was all there. The room was so quiet she could almost hear her heart beating.

"The garden is planted," she said. "Eighteen roses red, stocks of blue, hollyhocks and primrose, sweet William two." She heard a man at the table gasp.

She continued. "Canterbury bells with lilies white. Rows of carrots and cabbages to greet the light."

The officer touched the fabric with his finger. "And these?" he asked.

"A row of bleeding hearts," Anne said primly. "To confuse the enemy."

The officer smiled.

No one spoke. Anne looked about the table. The men sat, stunned.

"What does it mean?" Adam asked.

The officer smiled at Adam. "Your sister and her code will help us save the day. It's simple." He leaned over and pointed to the stitching.

"Eighteen roses red are 18,000 grenadiers."

Adam sucked in his breath.

"Stocks of blue. They're on the move."

Anne gasped. That's why Ben had to hurry!

"Hollyhocks and primrose means two columns. One to Middlebush, and one to Somerset."

"They mean to try to get us out onto the plains," a man said.

"Aye," the officer answered. "It's where they fight the best." He smiled. "But now we can outfox them."

"The sweet Williams?" Anne asked.

The officer snorted. "General William Howe himself is at their lead. The Canterbury bells and lilies white mean he's traveling light."

"Probably left the flat bottom boats and portable bridge behind," one of the men said.

"Good!" said another officer.

"The rows of carrots and cabbages mean our spy ring is now complete." He smiled. "And we all know about the bleeding hearts." Then he sobered. "A good choice, my dear. There are many who grieve."

No one spoke. They all seemed deep in thought. And then Adam broke the silence. "Anne. What a marvelous thing you've wrought. A code. I never would have believed it."

Anne smiled. Adam gazed at her in wonder.

She turned to the officer. "Sir," she said. "I'd be obliged if you'd give the message to General Washington."

A man who was seated at the center of the table stood. Anne looked up. He was tall, taller than Ben, and broad shouldered. He smiled. "I am General Washington."

Anne held her breath and then quickly curtsied. Adam stood stunned.

"You've done a brave deed to bring us this news." The general looked her over carefully, and she blushed as she thought of her torn dress.

"This deed deserves a reward," he said. "Do you have any requests?"

She looked at the stitchery. General Washington followed her gaze and picked up the dirtied linen. "Not worth much to look at, but I suggest you save it for your grandchildren." He handed it to Anne. "And what else?"

Anne frowned. Suddenly, her thoughts of getting linen for a coverlet seemed petty. There were more important things to ask for. She looked at Adam. He wanted desperately to be a soldier, but he was needed at home. "Sir," she said quietly. "My brother. We've no one to do the plowing or planting."

Washington nodded. "And we've a hungry army." He looked at Adam. "Son, if you can farm as good as I hear you soldier, this army will be well fed."

"That I can, sir. But..." He paused. "Well, I'd fancied myself a soldier in your army."

Washington smiled. "Your sister has no uniform, no musket, and yet she has soldiered better than I probably ever shall. Son, there are other ways to care for your country. Go home and farm. You can come back again next winter. We will have need of you then."

Washington walked up to Anne and took her hand. "Thank you, my dear. What's your name?"

Anne curtsied again. "I'm Anne Elizabeth Brewster."

"Well, I shall tell the company today that Anne Elizabeth Brewster brought us information that will help us defeat this enemy." He paused. "Pray for us," he said quietly. "We will need it. This war is only beginning. But we will prevail." He turned and went back to his seat.

The officer at the end of the table spoke. "Miss, stay and rest. Your brother can take you home tomorrow."

"But, sir, I need to hurry home to my mother. I promised."

He smiled. "Very well. Brewster, prepare to leave at once. And take good care of this young lady."

"Aye, sir. That I will."

Anne looked at Adam. "You may accompany me, but I assure you I can look after myself."

The men chuckled.

Adam grinned. "Let's go." He held the tent flap for her. "You are a wonder, Annie. A code. My mates will be amazed. Who ever would have thought?"

Adam hurried to his tent to get his gear. He had to tell everyone about the code. The men gathered around Anne, offering her cups of hot water and bits of dried bread, and asking for news of home. She said little. Her heart was too heavy with her memories of Ben and Morgan.

Finally, they were on their way. "And did you see Morgan in town?" Adam asked. He grinned.

Anne stopped. "No more, Adam. No more teasing about Morgan. Not ever again."

"Oh, Annie. 'Tis only a jest."

Anne looked toward New Brunswick. "You'll need to find other ways to jest with me." Her voice was choked with emotion. "I'll not tolerate that teasing."

Adam put his hand on her shoulder. "Anne, what is it? What's happened?"

Anne shook her head. "I don't want to talk about it yet." She started walking. "Let's go. Mama will be worried."

15
Home Again

Adam led Anne to the river, and to a boat hidden on the bank. He plied her with questions about her journey as he rowed, but she wasn't ready to talk. "Later," she told him. "After we get home." She feared telling him about Ben. Adam might do something rash. She'd wait till they were home with Mama. At the thought of home tears smarted her eyes. It would be so good to be home. She vowed she'd never complain ever again.

The boat hit the far shore with a soft thud. "Let's stop at the Widow's," Anne said. "I want to be sure she's all right."

They hurried through the streets until they were at the Widow's house. Adam banged on the door. "I hear she's getting deaf," he said.

Anne smiled.

There was no answer. Anne peeked in the windows. The fire was burning brightly. A good sign.

"She's probably out visiting," Adam said. "She's the worst kind of gossip." He started down the street. "Come on."

Anne pounded on the door again and waited. She longed to tell the Widow she'd gotten the message to Washington. She sighed. It would have to wait. She turned to join Adam.

"Anne! Anne Elizabeth!"

Anne turned. It was Morgan, running down the street. Her heart jumped.

He rushed up to her. "I've been haunting this street," Morgan panted, "hoping you'd come by again."

"I was just checking to see about the Widow."

"She's fine," Morgan said. "Probably out visiting."

Adam joined them.

"Anne," Morgan said. "I've been thinking about when we last talked." He looked at Adam. "Uh, Adam, uh...this is private. Could you...?"

Adam frowned and then smiled. "Aye. Take your time." He walked away, whistling loudly.

Morgan waited a moment and then said, "I've little time for they are loading our belongings and we leave on the tide."

Anne felt her heart sink.

"I've been thinking. You see, I'm not the first son and so I'll have no inheritance. But I do believe your father was right, that there is something here in this new land for me. I know not what it is, but I know it is here, where you are." He paused. "I'll learn a worthwhile trade, I promise. And when I reach my majority I'm coming back."

"Here?" Anne asked.

He nodded and took her hand. "Dare I ask? It's only two years away. Will you wait for me?"

"But what about Faith?"

Morgan frowned. "Faith?"

"Yes. I thought you and Faith..."

Morgan shook his head. "No, we're just friends. That's all we've ever been. It's you, Anne."

Anne's face warmed.

"Will you wait?" he asked. "I know I have little to offer, but..."

She swallowed for she didn't trust her voice. "Yes."

"And write? Will you?"

Anne nodded.

"I must go." He squeezed her hand and then kissed her lips.

A hot feeling flared through Anne.

Morgan looked at her and then dropped her hand. He reached into a pocket and frowned. Then he looked down at the silver buttons on his waistcoat. Quickly, he tore one loose and handed it to Anne. "It's all I have for now. But keep it, so you won't forget me. It's my promise to you."

Anne closed her fingers about the button. "I won't forget you." Tears began to fill her eyes.

He squeezed her hand again. "Remember now. You'll wait." He called out to Adam as he ran away. "You take good care of her."

Adam grinned.

Anne looked at the button. Carved into the silver was a pattern of intersecting circles. She tucked it into her pocket beside the horse chestnut.

Adam and Anne were silent on the way home. Anne didn't want to disturb her memories of Morgan, and Adam seemed to understand.

The sun was just setting as they walked down the path to the farm. "Mama," Adam shouted.

The door opened and Mama peeked out. She saw them and raised her apron to her face. And then she ran toward them. She hugged Anne and then Adam. Then she hugged them both again. Soon they were in the house.

Anne rushed to the young soldier's bedside. His eyes were open and he raised himself onto his arm.

"I'm back," Anne said. "I delivered the message to the general."

The young man sighed and fell back onto the pillow. "Thank you," he whispered, and his eyes closed.

Anne looked at her mother. "Is he...?"

"He's still burning with fever, but he'll recover."

Adam frowned. "Who is he? Where's he from?"

"New York," Mama said. "He told me this morning when he had a clear moment. It was his first. He has two brothers in the Rebel army—with Washington—and a sister at home."

"Maybe I know them," Adam said.

Mama tucked the blanket around the soldier's body. "There will be plenty of time to find out when he's better." She looked at Anne. "I don't know what to think." Tears came to her eyes. "Ben sent word that he had seen you and would bring you home shortly. I was so angry and frightened when I realized you'd gone." Her voice became choked. "Don't you ever do anything like that again, you hear?"

Anne hugged Mama. "I'm sorry, Mama, but I had to go. I just had to."

Mama blew her nose into a large white square. "Well, what's done is done." She reached over and touched Adam's face. "And here's our Adam, home safe and sound. You've been sorely missed, son."

Adam smiled shyly. "The general said I could come back to the army next winter."

"In due time," Mama said. "But come, we'll have something to eat. You must be starving."

Mama served them hot gruel and corncakes and insisted they tell her everything.

Tears filled Anne's eyes for she had wonderful news to tell, and terrible news. She spread the stitchery on the table and they stared at it in silence.

"Tell about the code," Adam said.

"So there was a code," Mama whispered. She looked at Anne. "Tell us everything, dear."

Anne told them about the Widow and of her adventures getting to the Rebel camp. Mama's eyes were wide with wonder. "And did you get to see Washington?"

Anne nodded. "He's a big man, tall and broad, and a fine gentleman. He let Adam come home to do the plowing."

Mama wiped her eyes with the corner of her apron. "God grant he end these troubles quickly."

Anne paused and then said quietly, "Mama, Ben's a Loyalist."

Mama nodded thoughtfully. "I thought he might be."

"Fool!" Adam said.

"Watch your tongue, son," Mama said. "He's still your brother."

"He's no brother of mine. Not anymore. I'll never say his name again."

Mama began to cry. Anne's heart sank. Would they ever be a family again? She certainly hoped so. She said nothing about Morgan. Not yet. She wanted to savor the feelings all by herself. Some day soon she'd tell, but not yet.

Mama rose and took Anne's chin in her hand. "You look different, somehow."

Anne smiled. "I've grown up, Mama."

Mama picked up the stitchery. "If I wash it carefully it will do for framing. What was it the general said?"

"For my grandchildren." Anne smiled and hugged her mother. "We'd best go to bed. Lots to do tomorrow."

Adam nodded. "Aye. I'll go get a horse from Mistress McNabb. We can start the plowing."

Anne smiled. She took the silver button from her pocket and looked at it. She'd find a ribbon, dark brown like Morgan's eyes, and wear it about her neck. What would happen in the future, she had no idea, but now she felt ready to face it.

Author's note: The facts revealed in the code are accurate. Anne Brewster and her family, along with the code and the stitchery, are figments of the author's imagination. However, there were many young girls and boys performing courageous deeds in those days just as they do today.

Bibliography

Newspapers

Boston Gazette

The Essex Gazette

The Instructor printed by Benjamin Franklin

Maryland Gazette

Maryland Journal

The Massachusetts Gazette & Weekly Newsletter

New York Gazette

New York Journal

New York Mercury

Pennsylvania Chronicle

Pennsylvania Gazette

Pennsylvania Packet

South Carolina Gazette & Country Journal

Virginia Gazette

Adult Books

Bakeless, John. 1959. *Turncoats, Traitors & Heroes.*

Bruce, Elizabeth St. John and Edith Stinson Jones. 1970. *The Plimoth Colony Cook Book.*

Child, Mrs. 1832. *The American Frugal Housewife.*

De Pauw, Linda Grant. 1974. *Four Traditions: Women of New York During the American Revolution.*

Dolan, Jay P. (Editor). 1976. *Heritage of '76.*

Hatch, Charles E. Jr. 1957. *Yorktown and the Siege of 1781.*

Jakes, John. 1977. *The Bastard.*

———. 1978. *The Rebels.*

Lane, Rose Wilder. 1963. *Woman's Day Book of American Needlework.*

Langguth, A. J. 1988. *Patriots: The Men Who Started the American Revolution.*

Leckie, Robert. 1992. *George Washington's War: The Saga of the American Revolution.*

Martin, Joseph Plumb. 2001. *A Narrative of a Revolutionary Soldier: Some of the Adventures, Dangers, and Sufferings of Joseph Plumb Martin* (originally published as "Private Yankee Doodle" written by Martin in his old age).

Morgan, Edmund S. 1956. *The Birth of the Republic.*

Morison, Samuel Eliot. 1972. *The Oxford History of the American People, Volume I, Prehistory to 1789.*

Paine, Thomas. 1776/1986. *Common Sense.*

Phillips, Robert & Martyn Rix. 1991. *The Random House Book of Perennials.*

Riley, Edward M. 1956. *Independence.*

Rossiter, Clinton. 1963. *The Political Thought of the American Revolution.*

Scheer, George F. and Hugh F. Rankin. 1957. *Rebels and Redcoats.*

Symonds, Craig L. 1986. *A Battlefield Atlas of the American Revolution.*

Taylor, Dale. 1997. *Everyday Life in Colonial America.*

Thornwell, Emily. 1856/1984. *The Lady's Guide to Perfect Gentility.*

U.S. Government Printing Office. 1969. *Inaugural Addresses of the Presidents of the United States from George Washington 1789 to Richard Milhous Nixon.*

Vaughan, Alden T. (Editor). 1967. *America Before the Revolution 1725-1775.*

Wesley, John. 1755/1973. *Primitive Remedies* (originally *Primitive Physick*).

Wilson, Vincent Jr. (Editor). 1983. *The Book of Great American Documents.*

Children's Books

Adler, David A. 1991. *A Picture Book of Thomas Jefferson.*

Beller, Susan. 2003. *Yankee Doodle and the Redcoat.*

Benchley, Nathaniel. 1969. *Sam the Minuteman.*

Brenner, Barbara. 1994. *If You Were There in 1776.*

Cipriano, Jeri. 1998. *Colonial Times.*

Collier, James Lincoln. 1989. *My Brother Sam Is Dead.*

Denenberg, Barry. 1998. *The Journal of William Thomas Emerson: A Revolutionary War Patriot.*

Forbes, Esther. 1943. *Johnny Tremain.*

Fradin, Dennis. 1988. *The Thirteen Colonies.*

Fritz, Jean. 1969. *George Washington's Breakfast.*

————. 1973. *And Then What Happened, Paul Revere?*

Fritz, Jean. 1975. *Where Was Patrick Henry on the 29th of May?*

———. 1977. *Can't You Make Them Behave, King George?*

———. 1987. *Shh! We're Writing the Constitution.*

———. 1992. *George Washington's Mother.*

———. 1999. *Why Not LaFayette?*

Gilman, Dorothy. 1963. *The Bells of Freedom.*

Gregory, Kristiana. 1996. *The Winter of Red Snow: The Revolutionary War Diary of Abigail Jane Stewart, Valley Forge, 1777.*

———. 2001. *Five Smooth Stones: Hope's Revolutionary War Diary.*

Haykim, Joy. 1999. *From Colonies to Country (Book 3).*

Herbert, Janis. 2002. *The American Revolution for Kids.*

Keehn, Sally M. 1995. *Moon of Two Dark Horses.*

Knight, James E. 1998. *Boston Tea Party.*

———. 1982. *The Winter at Valley Forge.*

Krensky, Stephen. 2002. *Benjamin Franklin and His First Kite.*

Marzollo, Jean. 1994. *In 1776.*

McGovern, Ann. 1999. *The Secret Soldier: The Story of Deborah Sampson.*

Murray, Stuart. 1999. *America's Song: The Story of Yankee Doodle.*

O'Dell, Scott. 1991. *Sarah Bishop.*

Osborne, Mary Pope. 2000. *Revolutionary War on Wednesday.*

Roop, Peter and Connie Roop. 1986. *Buttons for General Washington.*

Stein, R. Conrad. 1995. *The Declaration of Independence.*

Tripp, Valerie. 1992. *Felicity: An American Girl.*

Waters, Kate. 1989. *Sarah Morton's Day: A Day in the Life of a Pilgrim Girl.*

Wood-Brady, Esther. 1993. *Toliver's Secret.*

Woodruss, Elvira. 1993. *George Washington's Socks.*

Wroble, Lisa A. *Kids in Colonial Times.*

Maps

C. S. Hammond & Company. 1953. *Historical Atlas.*

Miller, Theodore. 1969. *Graphic History of the Americas.*

United States Department of the Interior. *Maps.*

Wesley, Edgar. 1961. *Our United States: Its History in Maps.*

Educational Resources

The Revolutionary War

Trouble had been brewing long before the Declaration of Independence was signed in 1776. A long history of incidents, insults, and misunderstandings preceded that day.

There were several forces underlying the events leading to the rebellion. One was economic. The colonies during the early 1700s had suffered economic losses. The many unemployed men, who were a volatile force, were ready to riot for any reason as an outlet for their rage and anger. As only wealthy landowners were able to vote, the poor paid little attention to the politicians. They were interested in freedom only if it provided them with work. By the 1760s, even the wealthy began to feel the economic pinch of the taxes imposed on the colonies by Britain.

Another force was the lack of civil police forces in the colonies. Villages and towns enacted laws and did their best to manage. There were a few British soldiers, but they were not called upon to handle civil matters. This meant that if a riot began, it could not be squelched, as the local leaders were reluctant to use British army force. Samuel Adams soon learned the power of the mob. In the 1760s the citizens knew that a riot often got them what they wanted. So, clever men began writing and speaking about the incidents of the times in ways to promote their cause and incite rebellion. They became brilliant propaganda writers.

Their original plan had nothing to do with gaining freedom. Two goals existed: one to seek the repeal of the oppressive acts of Parliament and the other to find the proper place for the colonies in the British Empire.

Britain had used taxation as a way of controlling trade. However, by the 1760s Britain had incurred a huge debt and began using taxation as a way of raising money. This was what James Otis and Samuel Adams had been waiting for. Now they could claim the colonies were being taxed without being represented. The more the British Parliament tried to suppress the colonists, the more they fought for their freedom.

We are fortunate that the men and women in the New World were intelligent, thinking people. They used their understanding of history, their knowledge of politics, and their understanding of human behavior and needs to help create what would become the United States of America.

The Code

General Washington's army was small and lacking in proper equipment. It was vital that at this particular time he not engage the British army face-to-face on the open plain for the British army was made up of soldiers who were well trained and well equipped. The British army was considered to be the finest in the world.

Activity:

Design a code to carry the following information:

There are 18,000 grenadiers (British infantrymen) who are moving in two columns, one to Middlebush and one to Somerset. General William Howe is in charge. Because he needs to move quickly he has left the flat bottom boats and portable bridge behind. Also, a spy ring is now in place.

Medicine and Health

It's very easy for us now to laugh at the cures that Mistress Brewster was using to heal the young rebel soldier. Mistress Brewster was doing the very best she could with the information that was available at the time.

Mistress Brewster may have had a book called *Primitive Physick* (which meant Basic Medical Care) that was written by John Wesley, a famous reformer, evangelist, and the founder of the Methodist church. Wesley had attended the University at Oxford and was very interested in science, but he was opposed to many of the medical practices of the day such as using poisonous drugs and bleeding. He believed in the virtues of simple, natural remedies and the importance of maintaining good basic health.

Anne's father had read the essays of Dr. Benjamin Rush, published in 1771, on the evils of slavery, health, and temperance (he recommended moderation in all things). Rush was a well-known physician who was very involved in the fight for freedom for the colonies. He was a member of the provincial conference of

112

Pennsylvania, and chairman of the committee that believed it had become necessary for Congress to declare independence. He showed his enthusiasm for the colonial cause by riding out to meet the Massachusetts delegates to the first Continental Congress in 1774. He might have gone out to greet Malcolm Drew who was going to work with the Continental Congress. On July 4, 1776, Dr. Rush was one of the signers of the Declaration of Independence.

Although Mistress Brewster read only a little, her husband would have read to her. One of the favorite activities in Anne's family was to sit by the fire in the evening and have Mr. Brewster read to them. Anne liked to read and so would have read everything she could find.

One of Dr. Rush's "cures" advised that plunging a hot poker into vinegar will cause fumes to rise. These fumes reduce the danger of contagion during sickness. Mistress Brewster used a different "cure." She burned sulfur (spelled "sulphur" in Anne's day) to clean the contagion from the air. It was believed that "bad" air caused many diseases. It is one of the reasons people avoided going out at night as the "night vapors" were considered dangerous.

Other health/medical advice:

- ◆ Cure for baldness: Rub the part mornings and evenings with onions, till it is red, and rub it afterwards with honey.

- ◆ Cure for lethargy: Sniff strong vinegar up the nose. (Warning: Don't fall asleep in class!)

- ◆ Cure for a cold: Drink a pint of cold water lying down in bed.

o Or add one spoonful of molasses in half a pint of water.

o Or, to one spoonful of oatmeal, and one spoonful of honey add a piece of butter the bigness of a nutmeg; pour on, gradually, near a pint of boiling water. Drink this lying down in bed.

◆ Cure for a cold in the head: Pare very thin the yellow rind of an orange, roll it up inside out, and thrust a roll into each nostril.

Discussion questions:

◆ Why didn't Mistress Brewster call the doctor?

◆ What kind of medical practices do you have in your family? (Discuss Western and Eastern views of health and medicine.)

◆ How do you stay well? (Discuss "home" remedies the children may know about.)

◆ What would you do for the wounded soldier?

◆ What kind of information/training about emergencies should we have today?
o CPR
o Water safety
o Earthquake/tornado/hurricane
o Accident

◆ What do you think medicine will be like 200 years from today? What cures will we have that we do not have now?

Food, Cooking, Kitchens

Discussion questions:

- What would your family be eating if you had no refrigerator?

- What if you had no market?

- What would you grow in your garden?

- What foods were available to Anne's family? How were they prepared?

- What if you had no stove and had to cook everything using a fireplace. What would be your favorite foods?

- Anne's family would buy a ten-pound loaf of sugar that would last them all year. How much sugar do you eat in a year? In a day?

- Instead of sugar Anne's mother used honey, molasses, and sorghum. What is molasses? Where does it come from?

- How did General Washington feed his army?

o   The army bought food from a "sutler." This was a person who went about the countryside buying food. He would then sell it to the army. However, hungry armies don't always wait to buy the food but will steal whatever they can. This was a hardship on the people. So General Washington did all that he could to see that his army was taken care of. Sometimes this was extremely difficult as the Congress was very slow in giving him money. What happened at Valley Forge is an example of what happens when the army runs out of money. The Pennsylvania Assembly scolded Washington unjustly for going to winter at Valley Forge. They thought his army was twice the size it was and that he should have fought General Howe in Philadelphia. But Washington knew the limits of his army and was unwilling to risk lives.

Washington rarely lost his temper, however this time the politicians had gone too far. Washington responded: "The gentlemen reprobate the going into winter quarters as much as if they thought the soldiers were made of sticks or stones. I can assure these gentlemen that it is a much easier and less distressing thing to draw remonstrances in a comfortable room, than to occupy a cold bleak hill, and sleep under frost and snow without clothes or blankets. However, al-though they seem to have little feeling for the naked and distressed soldiers, I feel super-abundantly for them, and from my soul I Pity their miseries which it is neither in my power to relieve or prevent."[1]

---

1.   *George Washington's War*, pp. 433–34.

The Brewsters' diet consisted of:

◆ Fish from local rivers and streams

◆ Meats, poultry, and game
  o Venison
  o Wild fowl
  o Pigs
  o Goats
  o Sheep

◆ Cows were too valuable to slaughter for food. They were used for milk.

◆ Eggs. When a hen got old they would kill it and eat it.

◆ By spring their store of food would be low, with just some potatoes, beans, hard squashes, pumpkins, dried fruits, and apples.

◆ Corn was dried in the husk and hulled only when needed.

◆ Wheat, barley, oats, and rye.

◆ During the summer and fall they ate from their garden—vegetables and fruits.

◆ Wild berries. Eaten when fresh and also dried for the winter.

A poem from about 1630...

"If fresh meat is wanting to fill up our dish
We have carrots and turnips whenever we wish.
For pottage and puddings and custards and pies
Our pumpkins and parsnips are common supplies;
We have pumpkins at morning and pumpkins at noon,
It 'twere not for pumpkins we should be undone."[2]

---

2. *The Plimoth Colony Cook Book*, p. 37.

A well-equipped kitchen contained:

6 kettles, 3 iron pots, and a dripping pan
7 pewter platters, 3 great ones and 4 little ones
1 small mortar and pestle
4 pewter candlesticks
1 pewter flagon (a container for liquids), 4 pewter cups
1 beaker (broad glass container like a pitcher)
1 dram cup and a little bottle
2 salt sellers
3 porringers (a bowl for porridge)
6 old spoons
3 pair of pothooks
1 pair of tongs and an old fire shovel
1 pair of pot hangers
2 small iron hooks
1 pair of andirons
1 pressing iron
2 basins, one small and one great
wooden peel

Anne would have used a peel to put the coals into the oven and to take the food out. They were made of iron or wood and looked like what is used to take a pizza out of an oven. They are like a shovel with a long handle. The story is told that during King Philip's War, a lonely woman used a peel to defend herself from a warring Indian when he broke into her home. In the encounter he was killed.

Early brick oven

The early brick oven had no flue. It was set in the back of the fireplace, and the fire was built in the oven itself. The smoke came out of the open mouth and went up the main chimney. When the oven was thoroughly heated, the fire was removed, the food put in, and the oven door closed to retain the heat. The usual door was of heavy wood, made to fit the mouth of the oven and furnished with a handle by which it could be set in place.

To use the oven you had to first build a fire using kindling wood, then fairly dry wood. "It will take about five logs. At the end of about two hours, when the inside top of the oven is white and glowing, rake out the embers, and put in the prepared food. At the back, put the beans, which will stay overnight; the bread, pies, etc. go in the front. Close the oven door. When it is time to remove the food that needs the least amount of cooking, do so quickly so the oven does not cool. Close the door immediately."[3]

Fireplace equipment

A <u>lugstick</u> was a stick of green wood, supported by "lugs" or projections partway up the chimney. From this hung the pothooks by which the pots and kettles were suspended over the fire. You had to be sure to replace the lugstick before it charred, for if it broke, the kettles would spill and splash burning hot liquid on those who were nearby.

A <u>trammel</u> was an over-size pothook, hung on the lugstick. It had an adjustable linked shank which could be hung at various levels on the notched edge, so the cooking pot could be hung higher or lower over the fire.

Anne's mother also had a <u>swinging crane</u> in her fireplace. It was attached to the inside of the chimney and was hinged so it could swing to and fro. This allowed her to swing a heavy pot out of the fire so

---

3. *The Plimoth Colony Cook Book*, p. 7.

she could season her soup without burning her face or getting smoke in her eyes.

Mills

Before there was a mill in nearby New Brunswick, Anne and her mother ground their own meal.

Activity

If possible, try to make one of the following simpler recipes—seed cakes or Johnnycake.

Recipes (Mistress Brewster called them "receipts.")

Bean Porridge

"Bean porridge hot, bean porridge cold,
Bean porridge in the pot, nine days old.
Some like it hot, some like it cold;
Some like it in the pot, nine days old."[4]

These early settlers ate beans every day and sometimes at every meal. Anne's mother's recipe:

4 quarts of liquid (from beef or fowl if possible)
½ cup cornmeal
2 cups white beans that have been soaked over night
2 cups of hulled corn (dried)

Get broth to near boiling. Stir in the cornmeal slowly, stirring constantly. Then add the beans (cold baked beans can be used). When the beans begin to soften, add hulled corn and boil another ½ hour.

During a cold winter, the pioneers would put a loop of string in the porridge and then freeze it. These strings were hung up in a storage shed or barn, for if it was left outside, a wandering "critter" might take off with it. This frozen porridge and frozen chowder were

---

4. Old Nursery Rhyme.

convenient for men working in the woods. They could carry a loop of frozen porridge or chowder with them. When they got hungry they then put it in a pot over a fire and boiled it. Beans were always considered to be better after nine days.

Pease Porridge

By this time in history, gardeners in England had developed over 1000 varieties of peas! The colonists ate lots of peas—mostly dried. Thus we have this old nursery rhyme:

"Pease porridge hot, Pease porridge cold,
Pease porridge in the pot, nine days old.
Some like it hot, some like it cold;
Some like it in the pot, nine days old."

Both baked beans and pease porridge tasted better on the second day. We have no records of how they tasted on the ninth!

Many **types of chowder** were made using any kind of fish or shellfish, corn, and potatoes.

Soups were made out of anything and everything. Even cucumbers were made into a soup.

2 cups pared and diced cucumbers
½ cup soft butter
4 cups of chicken stock
¼ cup flour
1 slice onion
2 cups hot milk
salt and pepper

Cover the cucumbers with water and parboil them for 10 minutes. (The Brewsters probably had one clock in the house. Mistress Brewster learned to use her eyes and her nose when she cooked.) Drain. Add chicken stock and onion and cook until soft. Rub through a sieve. Blend butter and flour, and add to the soup, stirring constantly, while cooking, until slightly thickened. Season to taste and add hot milk. Strain and serve. Makes 6–8 servings.

This would have been a delicacy served for special occasions.

Toad in the Hole (a favorite English meal)

1 pound beef steak
2 cups milk
1 egg
1 cup flour
salt and pepper

Cut meat in small pieces and place in a well-greased baking dish. Beat egg, add milk, beat in flour and seasonings. Pour over meat and bake 1 hour (in a moderate oven of 350 degrees). Cooked meat can be used. Makes 3–4 servings.

Bubble and Squeak (another favorite)

"When midst the frying pan in accents savage,
The beef so surly quarrels with the cabbage."

This is generally made with slices of cold boiled beef, salted and sprinkled with a little pepper, then lightly browned in a frying pan. The cabbage is cut up, boiled until tender, then squeezed dry and chopped fine. Remove beef from the pan, add cabbage and heat through, stirring constantly. Lay the cabbage in the middle of a serving platter, and place the meat around it.

Indian Nokake (also called Johnnycake)

This is a recipe the settlers learned from the Indians. Roger Williams describes traveling through the woods with a group of Indians, "…every man carrying a little basket of Nokake at his back, sufficient for a man three or four days. With a spoonful of this meal, and a spoonful of water from a brook, have I made many a good dinner and supper."[5]

The name "Johnnycake" is probably a corruption of "Journey Cake."

Desserts and sweets (There were very few sweets for Anne)

"There being no sugar cane in that country, those trees (maples) supplied that liquor, which being boiled up and evaporated turned to a kind of sugar somewhat brownish but very good."[6]

Seed Cakes (These are the cakes that Maybelle liked)

Take one pound of sugar and as much flour; a pound of butter (or fat) washed in rose water. Drain the butter. Add four eggs and a few drops of cinnamon oil and some ground nutmeg. Crush a good handful of caraway seeds. (Anne's mother would have said, "bruise them.") Mix all together and then drop them in lumps as big as a nutmeg upon a buttered tin. Bake them in a crisp oven. Then dry them until they are crisp.

Corn pudding (another favorite)

"Five kernels of corn in a row,
One for the blackbird, one for the crow,
One for the cutworm and two to grow!"[7]

1 egg
½ teaspoon sugar (or molasses)

5. *The Plimoth Colony Cook Book*, p. 47.
6. Joutel (1687) From *The Plimoth Colony Cook Book*, p. 55.
7. Common rhyme from the times.

1 cup milk
½ tablespoon melted butter
½ teaspoon salt
few grains of cayenne pepper
1 cup cooked corn, scraped from the cob

Beat the egg, add milk, seasonings, butter, and corn. Turn into a buttered baking dish and bake (350 degrees in a modern oven) about 45 minutes or until center is firm like a custard. Serves 4.

Loblolly

Women used whatever "flour" they had (corn, rye, wheat, other grains) and ground it very fine. They added it to boiling milk along with some kind of sweetener like maple sugar, honey, or molasses. If they had any fruit, it was added. They then cooked the mixture until it was thick.

An old Plymouth Colony receipt (recipe) says: "Take the morning's milk and throw into it as much cornmeal as you can hold in the palm of your hand. Let the molasses drip in as you sing 'Nearer My God to Thee,' but sing two verses in cold weather."[8]

Hasty Pudding

This was merely 6 cups of rapidly boiling water to which you add 1 cup of cornmeal and a teaspoon of salt. It was served hot with molasses and milk, or sugar and butter and nutmeg. 8 servings.

Discussion Questions:

◆ How could the colonists preserve their food?

◆ How do we do it now?

---

8. *The Plimoth Colony Cook Book*. p. 50.

Cookbooks

Anne's mother had these cookbooks brought over from England by her mother.

The Queen's Closet Opened. London, 1671.

> *Imcomparable secrets in Physick, Chirurgery, Preserving, and Candying, etc., which are presented unto the Queen By the most Experienced Persons of the Times, many of whom were held in esteem, when She pleased to descend to private Recreations.*

The Compleat Cook. London, 1671.

> *Exactly Prescribing the Most Ready Wayes whether Italian, Spanish, French, For dressing of Flesh or Fish, ordering of Sauces or making of Pastry.*

Clothing

Discussion questions:

◆ What would you be wearing if you had to make your clothes, sew them by hand and even weave the fabric?

◆ How are your clothes made? Where are they made? (If appropriate, introduce the controversy over foreign-made clothing.)

◆ Anne had two dresses. How many pieces of clothing do you have?

Educational Resources
References

Bruce, Elizabeth St. John, and Edith Stinson Jones, comps. *The Plimoth Colony Cook Book*. Plymouth, Massachusetts: Plymouth Antiquarian Society, 1957/1970.

Leckie, Robert. *George Washington's War: The Saga of the American Revolution*. New York: HarperPerenial, 1992.

Wesley, John. *Primitive Physick: or, An Easy and Natural Method of Curing Most Diseases*. London: R. Hawes, 1776.

— The Author —

Ruth H. Maxwell is an established author of children's books and short stories. She has written a syndicated column, *Revolutionary Times: 200 Years Ago Today*, and contributes to many magazines. A member of the Society of Children's Book Writers and Illustrators, her work is dedicated to making history come alive for children of today.

"Ruth Maxwell's well-researched details enrich the tapestry of danger and intrigue, placing us directly in the heart of young America. If Nancy Drew had been alive in 1774, her name would be Anne Brewster."
 —Terri Cohlene, Author of *Dancing Drum,*
  Something Special, and *Won't Papa Be Surprised!*

"A wonderful book. This exciting story kept me turning pages. It makes you feel like you have taken a time machine back to the days when ordinary girls and boys were becoming heroes as they helped to create our nation....destined to become a children's classic."
 —Cynthia Whitcomb, Author; Screenwriter for "Mark
  Twain and Me," *Wonderful World of Disney*

"...delivers a rich, yet terrifying account of events through the eyes of a young girl. Loaded with details true to the times...."
 —Patricia Mauser McCord, Award-winning Author of
  A Bundle of Sticks and *Pictures in the Dark*

"Readers will be caught up in this...dramatic story filled with historical events that enables us to relive a moment in our United States history."
 —Stacey Brody, Library Media Specialist

— Of Related Interest —

DIVIDED LOYALTIES
A Revolutionary War Fifer's Story
Phyllis Hall Haislip

The Revolutionary War has torn apart eleven-year-old Teddy's family. His father is a Patriot, his mother a Loyalist. Teddy mistakenly joins the wrong unit of the local regiment and enters a whole new world of men and boys headed off to war in faraway South Carolina. As a member of the fifes and drums, Teddy forges new loyalties and faces defeat at the Battle of Camden in August 1780.

ISBN-13: 978-1-57249-369-8 • Softcover

THE FORGOTTEN FLAG
Revolutionary Struggle in Connecticut
Frances Y. Evan

In 1964 a stained, old American flag is found in the attic rafters of a colonial farmhouse. The mystery of the flag's discovery is revealed as the story returns to the year 1779. *The Forgotten Flag* is the story of courage and sacrifice in a small community of ordinary townsfolk who make a stand against oppression and injustice.

ISBN-13: 1-57249-338-4 • Softcover

WHITE MANE PUBLISHING CO., INC.

To Request a Catalog Please Write to:
WHITE MANE PUBLISHING COMPANY, INC.
P.O. Box 708 • Shippensburg, PA 17257
e-mail: marketing@whitemane.com
Our Catalog is also available online
www.whitemane.com

CPSIA information can be obtained
at www.ICGtesting.com
Printed in the USA
FSOW03n2047280816
24324FS